REACH

THE TANDRO SERIES - A NOVELLA

NAOMI E LLOYD

Sarah,

with lots of love

[signature]
xxo

Dedicated to the memory of Irene Hartley, Enid Smith and Joan Russell.

Three great ladies: Irene and Enid, my biological grandmothers, and Joan, my grandmother by marriage.

It was because of you lovely ladies that I will always be mindful of:

Who I am, What I can do, and Where I come from.

And with thanks and devotion to my own diamond family:

Thank you for your patience and steadfast belief in me.

JOIN MY TANDRO DIAMOND TEAM

Naomi's Tandro Team members gain access to the exclusive Tandro Diamond Energy Cave for free books, treasure hunt competitions, behind the scene photographs and unique items to accompany the books.

Members are always the first to hear about Naomi's new books and publications.

See the back of the book to find details on how to sign up.

1

DREAMS

Her stomach heaved in response to the rocking motion of the ship as it battled to stay upright against the violent waves. It made her gag. The ice-cold wind knocked her sideways as she fought against it. Her nostrils flared wide as she breathed in the smell of extreme fear around her, a distinctive scent of sweat. The kind only those with advanced sensory abilities could detect.

A man in a dark blue uniform ran towards her, clutching a small child to his chest. He screamed at her to get into the lifeboat with the other women and children. Erin shouted out to him, pleading for answers. *Where were they? What was going on?* But the man ran straight past her. Any response he may have offered was now lost in the fog.

"Don't leave me!" Erin shouted to him.

Another man ran past her then, and the same pungent scent of terror filled her nose. She could just make out what he was wearing – a black tuxedo and white scarf – before he was lost in the thick mist that surrounded her.

There was no point reaching out to the man or anyone else caught up in this nightmare. She was not part of the dream in the same way they were. Yes, she was here with them, on this sinking ship, but she knew she would not escape on the lifeboats with them.

Someone else would appear soon. She always did. But Erin did not have the remote control to this dream. She could not fast forward it.

Erin reached her hand out to grab hold of a white pole. It was slippery from the onslaught of sideways rain, but she secured enough balance by thrusting her body against it and wrapping her left leg around the frigid metal.

As the storm howled around her, she closed her eyes, not wanting to think too much about the meaning behind her placement in this scene.

"Erin!" A female voice commanded her attention. She flashed her eyes open, searching for the direction it was coming from, but the fog made it impossible to see more than a foot in front of her.

"I'm here!" Erin called out. She knew this voice. It belonged to the girl with the diamond-shaped pupils and long, black bobbed hair. The same girl who had been conducting her dream prophecies as long as Erin could remember.

She knew the girl must be close by. The grey mist ahead of her had already transformed into a turquoise-coloured smoke. Erin called out again. Within seconds, the girl appeared before her, surrounded by a glow of green and blue light that concealed the details of her naked frame.

The girl frowned at the sight of Erin's shivering body still clinging to the pole. "Why are you shaking, Erin? You know you will wake up before you fall. You are not going to suffer in the disaster that strikes this ship."

The girl – who still looked to be in her early twenties and never seemed to age – seemed oblivious to the treacherous weather conditions they faced. With her arms folded, she stood before Erin at an angled but perfectly balanced position. It was as though she existed in another version of this scene, where the wind and rain had yet to commence their battle.

"You've never put me on a sinking ship before! Of course, I'm shaking," Erin hissed back at her. A part of her wanted to reach out to the girl and hit her, to order her to stop this nightmare. It was clear this dream was designed to test her resilience, but this was painful in a way none of the other dreams had been. This was terrifying!

The storm still raged. The frightened people continued to race past them as the ship sank into the waters. Erin was not sure her hands could keep hold on the pole for much longer. And by the way the ship was now positioned – almost on its side – she knew if she let go, she would fall into the ocean.

"Stop it!" Erin screamed. "I will listen to what you say, but stop this now! I can feel *everything*!"

The coloured mist glowed around the girl, more vibrant than Erin had ever seen it before. Brilliant light flashed from her diamond-shaped pupils, and her rich, amber-toned skin radiated a welcome heat as she moved her body closer to Erin's shivering frame.

"Are you sure you cannot hold on?" The girl's voice vibrated its question.

An animal-like noise erupted from Erin. It was a growl, a new sound she gladly directed at this dream-controlling apparition before her.

"I'm not superhuman. I don't have magical powers to stop me from falling! Why are you testing me like this? What does this dream warn about my future? To avoid travelling on ships? I don't understand!"

The girl smiled. The sound of her deep laughter carried across the wind before drifting away like mocking echoes.

"You are so like your mother, Erin. And the others before. If only you could remember who you are, what you can do, and where you come from, this would all be so much easier."

Erin growled at her again. She had heard this too many times before. It still didn't make any sense. She refused to warrant it with an answer.

"Get on it with already! What is the warning behind this dream?" Erin shouted back. The only sounds she could detect came from the frightened screams of passengers muffled by the howling of excitable winds dancing in the frenzy of the storm.

The girl seemed farther away now. Erin could no longer feel her heat.

Exhausted but determined, she squeezed her eyes tight and held her breath, willing the storm to die and the dream to reach an end.

Erin screamed again. Strength was not one of her natural attributes, but for some reason, her hands held their grip on the slippery pole despite the storm gaining momentum. She willed herself to keep holding on, but her legs had started to shake, and she was rapidly losing her resolve.

"Erin! Concentrate! Stay in the dream! You will miss the message if you drift away."

The girl's voice was nearer again now. Erin, eyes still closed, inhaled the distinctive scent of mint chocolate coming off the girl as she approached.

At last! she thought. Although the girl's smell was not one she liked, she always relished this moment in a dream. When the girl got this close, it usually signalled the dream's climax was near.

Erin opened her eyes, tears immediately filling them in reaction to the biting wind. She blinked in rapid succession, but it did little to clear her vision. She could only just make out the silhouette of the girl as she moved closer to her.

"I can't *see* you! Can you turn this storm off somehow? It's really starting to hurt! I can't hold on any longer!" Erin pleaded.

She had already decided. If this charade did not end soon, she would let go of the pole. Nothing bad would happen. As real as this dream felt, she had to keep telling herself that she wouldn't die in her sleep. If she let go, the dream would surely end.

She started to count down in her head. If she reached to zero, she would do it...she would let go.

10, 9, 8, 7...

Then, without warning, everything calmed. The wind died down, the waves stilled, and the fog cleared.

Erin looked down to check the ship's position. It was still lying at an angle but was now upright enough for her to relieve her clutch on the pole and lean against the wall close by.

"You almost let go! I'm glad you didn't."

Erin's head snapped up at the sound of a new voice in front of her. She gasped. The vision before her was still the girl, but she was now surrounded by a soft coral colour.

"You? But...who are you now? You look different," Erin managed to whisper.

The girl's face lit up with a warm smile as she reached her hand out to touch Erin's cheek. Her fingers caressed her skin in a circular motion. The soft, padded tips sent surges of warmth through her. It appeared this was a new version of the girl and one Erin instantly preferred.

It was subtle at first, the change – how the girl's eyes opened wider, and her lips appeared fuller. But then, as her hair grew longer and her shoulders relaxed, Erin felt herself being drawn towards her. Normally, she preferred to keep her distance from the dream girl.

Instinctively, Erin leaned forward to inhale the space between them. "You smell different too. Like grapefruit and lime and, erm... wood?" Erin suggested, her voice wavering.

Now that adrenaline no longer rushed through her veins she felt drained of all energy.

The girl nodded and touched both her cheeks with a gentle

pressure. Erin felt herself drifting away from this dream. She was desperate to wake up but not before she discovered

why she had been put through this ordeal in the first place!

"What was I supposed to take from this?" Erin pleaded, barely able to catch her breath.

The girl's expression turned sad then. She lowered her eyes and said, in a voice that was softer than Erin had ever heard before, "Remember, Erin, *everything* is breakable. You just have to find its weak point!"

Erin's mum swiped away her cereal bowl from under her before she had time to slurp up the chocolate milk. It was a childish habit Erin had yet to grow out of, even though she was nearly sixteen.

"Erin! Are you sure you are okay to get the tube to the hospital? Straight from school? No loitering around by the skate park this time!" her mum asked and instructed all in one rushed sentence.

"Hmm... yeah, okay!" Erin mumbled in response.

Running her two front teeth across her bottom lip whilst tapping her foot on the kitchen bar stool, she weighed up the benefits of telling her mum about the return of the dreams.

"Mum, are you in a mad rush? I mean, I know you are, but I just wanted to..." Erin stammered, unable to find the words to express the anxious feelings she was so desperate to release.

It was a stupid thing to ask her right now. Of course, her mum was in a rush. Stefanie Barrett's life was one big whirlwind of responsibility.

Erin yawned as she watched her mum hastily clearing the remaining evidence of the family breakfast from the kitchen table. As tempting as it was to ask for some motherly advice—particularly as she knew her mum shared her curse of psychic dreaming—she conceded that now was *not* a good time. Her mum had already broken a glass and was now carelessly dropping crockery into the sink. Erin sighed at the sound of her favourite cereal bowl smashing into pieces in the iron basin. Her mum didn't even flinch. Instead, she just growled at the destruction in front of her.

"Sorry, honey. I'll get you another one," Stefanie apologized in a distracted mumble.

Erin just shrugged at her. They both knew the bowl was unreplaceable. It was unlikely Disney still kept stock of their Christmas memorabilia from five years ago! "Yeah, there's always eBay," Erin offered.

Although her mum had her back to her, Erin could tell she was crying. Her shoulders shook, and her breathing had become laboured.

"What did you want to say?" Stefanie asked her, still leaning over the ceramic destruction she had created in the kitchen sink.

Erin had to fight back her own tears. Seeing her mum this upset was unbearable. Stefanie had always been the life and soul of their family. Now she was more like a bomb waiting to go off, a pent-up fireball of restrained energy that Erin did not want to be responsible for unleashing.

"It's nothing. I was just going to ask what we were doing this week-end," Erin finally answered.

She regretted the words immediately. Another stupid thing to ask. They would do what they always did now: visit her younger brother, Lyndon, in hospital.

Before her mum had chance to fire back an angry response, she added, "I meant, what are the visiting times? Just so I can factor in homework too."

Stefanie turned around to face her. She was all puffy-eyed and blotched skin but somehow still the prettiest mum Erin knew.

"Oh, Erin, honey. Look, it's okay. I know it doesn't feel like it, but me and your dad know you have a life too. We *do* have to prioritise Lyndon at the moment, but that doesn't mean we expect you to spend every moment at the hospital with us when you're not at school."

Stefanie managed a forced smile.

"Tell you what, why don't you come along to the hospital an hour later than normal after school finishes? I know you said Serenity and Liberty keep asking you to hang out with them, and you should. Go get an ice cream at that café you like on the South Bank. Just keep your phone on you, so I can get hold of you." Stefanie raised her eyebrows at her expectantly, waiting for Erin's agreement.

Erin nodded and managed to return an identical forced smile back to her mum.

"Sure, that'd be cool," Erin responded amiably.

There you go again, Erin! More lies!

How could she tell her mum that she despised spending time with her new school *friends,* Serenity and Liberty? There were few things worse than having to partake in their absurd make-up chatter. It was all such vacuous rubbish! Although, it did help to have alibis like them now that she had a secret to hide: a boyfriend. She knew her parents would disapprove of him—*if* she could call Kieran a *boyfriend,* that is!

"Erin, did you want to say anything else? It sounded like something was bothering you earlier. You haven't been having those strange dreams again, have you?" Stefanie dared. Her tone suggested she was afraid to hear her daughter's answer.

Erin bit her lip, unsure how she should reply. Just thinking of the icy temperatures and the desperate screams of the ship's passengers made her feel queasy. She wanted nothing more than to run into her mum's arms and say, "Yes, the dreams are back!" But she managed to quieten the urge. She needed to be stronger than that because the warning voice inside her head was much louder. The one that reminded her that everything is breakable if you find its weak point.

What is breakable? She nearly screamed out loud, but again, she stilled the rumblings of her frustrated thoughts, took a deep breath, and composed herself.

"Nah! That was just a weird stage I went through, Mum. I blame it on the horror movies I was obsessed with for a while," she finally answered.

Erin rolled her eyes in her mum's direction. A perfect expression to accompany a perfect lie.

Stefanie didn't look convinced.

"Mum! Really!" Erin reassured again.

"Okay, well, if you're sure, honey. Look, I really do have to make a move. I'm booked to see Dr. Green in less than an hour, and you know how bad traffic is getting to the hospital at this time of day." Stefanie rocked her body a little from side to side, as though unsure about the justification in her words.

"Mum! Just go, okay? I'll be fine. I want to do some more reading for this test before school, and Dad said one of the drivers will take me this morning. I'll see ya at the hospital later, then?"

As much as Erin hated the idea of being on her own around the city at the moment, she didn't want to miss the opportunity to see Kieran. He was the only part of her life that made her feel excited anymore - and free!

"Yep, that's fine. Like I said, you can hang out for an hour after school with the girls," Stefanie clarified, already making a move for the door.

Erin nodded, averting her gaze. She never used to lie to her mum like this, but these were desperate times. Stefanie needed to concentrate on getting Lyndon better. And it was Erin's responsibility to shield her from any extraneous burdens, to convince her that she was the child her mum didn't need to worry about.

"See ya! Say hi to Lynds for me!" she called out to her mum as Stefanie rushed out of the door.

Erin unclenched her fists, relieved by the silence her mum's departure had brought. She yawned again. The recent dreams were a pain in more than one way. Not only were they exhausting, but they didn't make any sense! How was she supposed to stop a ship from sinking? Things like that didn't happen anymore! Did they?

She tapped the screen of her phone, debating whether to Google the date when the Titanic sank. Was there something obvious she was missing, like a new version of the fated ship due to set sail?

"No point!" she reasoned out loud. It was obvious the diamond-eyed girl was playing with her. Placing her in a disaster dream scene had to be a test, a sadistic game to check if fifteen-year-old Erin was now old enough to pick up on her weird metaphors.

Her younger dreams had been so much easier to cope with. At least they had always suggested pleasant things were on the horizon, like her dad getting appointed as the U.S. ambassador in London. No one had believed her when she announced *that* would happen at a family dinner when they were still in Washington. Sure, Adam Barrett had an excellent political record, but he was much younger than the other, more obvious candidates. And yet, to everyone's surprise, her dad was offered the position only two weeks later!

Erin had never felt happier that she was gifted in this way! Although, when her mum then confessed she had *also* dream predicted events at a similar age Erin soon realised Stefanie's childhood dream prophecies had carried more global significance. Apparently, at the age of ten, Stefanie had predicted Nelson Mandela would one day become the President of South Africa. This, at a time when he was still being held as a political prisoner in the country!

"Crazy diamond girls"—that's what her dad had affectionately started calling them both after that, some music reference to seeing visions she still didn't quite get. It seemed ironic now she thought about it. Trust her dad to choose a nickname that related to diamonds, of all things! Maybe *he* had planted the crazy notions of diamond-eyed people in her head!

Erin groaned as she squeezed her eyes shut tight. At least predicting a new job position – or even a new President - was realistic. It was ridiculous to even contemplate that the dream girl, or girls, she saw when she closed her eyes at night would one day actually appear.

And yet, lately, she had the strangest feeling that they were more than just made-up characters in her dreams. That they could plague her, both when she was asleep and awake. Just the thought of it made her shudder.

"Get a life, Erin!" she growled out loud to herself. All this worrying about things that could never happen was just pointless and energy-draining. It was time to focus on things that *could* happen and would give her an energy boost, like meeting Kieran later!

Grabbing her phone, she clicked on the white ghost icon to open snapchat and quickly typed.

Meet you later? 4 pm? Usual place?

The words *"Kieran is typing"* flashed on the phone screen in an instant. Erin jiggled her bottom in her seat. Even anticipating his reply gave her butterflies. As soon as the notification that he had sent a message popped up, she clicked on it.

I'll be there! Hope you look as good as last time!

Erin sucked in her breath as she read Kieran's message.

"What does that mean? Charming!" she complained to her phone.

Without stopping to think it through, she typed her reply.

I'll do my best?

Five minutes passed as she stared at her phone. Nothing! Sighing, Erin picked up her rucksack and made her way into the huge, circular entrance hall way to locate the driver who was supposed to be transporting her to school. Within seconds, the sound of an engine rumbling to life outside confirmed the driver's arrival. Yawning once again, Erin was about to twist the door handle to the front door when a white picture frame sitting on the glass side-dresser caught her eye.

"What the hell?" she gasped.

The frame contained a hand-written poem inside it. She recognized it instantly. The writing was hers, from when she was probably about nine years old. Smiling to herself, Erin picked it up and read the poem out loud, ignoring the persistent grumble of the car engine outside.

Mum

By Erin Barrett

Mum, you are my hero,
as strong as a diamond.
You are one in a quadrillion
and as rare as a diamond.
You walk me to school
every day and put
a smile on my face.
I love you.
I love you
so much.
I am so grateful
you are my mum!

Erin shook her head in disbelief. "So weird," she whispered. It wasn't the sentiment of the words that surprised her- she felt moved by how strong her connection with her mum was back then—but the realization that these diamond-connected dreams must have been hidden deeper inside her for a lot longer than she had thought. And perhaps even more reassuring, that she had not always found them so frightening.

2

BRIDGES

He did not fit a classic idea of beauty—Kieran's features were just that little too wide-set—but he had that *something*. Erin had no idea why he captivated her in the way that he did. There were boys in her school that fit the more obvious description of cool boyfriend-type, but she didn't want any of them. Her eyes were permanently in search of Kieran. Even in her dreams —when she could rid the weird diamond-eyed girl from her subconsciousness—Kieran would make an appearance.

As she approached the steps up to the Millennium Bridge, she waved up to him from where he was staring at her, his gaze firmly locked into her movements. Perhaps it *was* his eyes that drew her to him? His pupils *were* captivating, the deep black circles much larger than any she had seen, as though they widened up when she approached him to let her into his soul.

Stop being so crazy, Erin!

She did have some crazy ideas sometimes. Her thoughts had become more abstract recently, like she was accessing another part of her that Kieran had somehow awoken inside her. At least she hoped it was her reaction to him and not to anything else more ominous that lingered in her fears.

"Well, hello there, girl!" Kieran mused as she threw her arms around him. His body stiffened at her touch.

"Oh, sorry. Are you okay?" Erin drew back. It was difficult to gauge the best way to approach him. Sometimes he seemed more amorous towards her than others.

Kieran frowned for a brief moment. But to her relief, as soon as the lines had furrowed on his forehead, they smoothed out, quickly replaced by a few crinkles around his eyes as a beaming smile spread across his face.

"Hey, yeah, I'm great! I just landed funny when I was skating the other night with the boys, that's all. You squeezed me a little tight around the bruises. But that's cool. I'm a big boy!" He laughed, pulling her back into his arms.

Erin breathed a sigh of relief before inhaling his musky smell where her head rested on his chest. She loved how he always wore his shirt with two buttons open, just enough to reveal the few hairs on his skin and a hint of toned muscle above his nipples.

"Is that the aftershave I bought you?" Erin gushed. It had taken her hours to select the perfect scent to match his natural aroma. Not that she didn't like the animal, leather-like smell he emitted - it was quite intoxicating – but she sensed a touch of masculine herb-based perfume would enhance it to perfection.

"Hmm... I guess it must be," he answered, his hands already squeezing the softer part of her skin above the waistline of her jeans. "How come you got changed? I was hoping you'd be wearing that cute school uniform, like you did last time," Kieran teased.

Erin responded with a shy laugh, which was quickly lost as her mouth buried into the cotton of his shirt. The cheeky tone in his voice did not escape her. It was obvious he enjoyed testing her reaction to his more provocative references.

"Do you have to go back to work soon?" she whispered, keen to divert attention from her choice of clothing. Her school uniform was tucked away in her backpack. The last thing she wanted was to attract more unapproving eyes from strangers—as they had done last time— by kissing an older guy in public. But Kieran didn't need to know that was the reason she had changed into jeans and a vest top before meeting him. He had made it clear how much he hated people thinking he was too old for her.

"What's the age difference between your mum and dad, then? Didn't you say it was thirteen years? Well, that's the same for us. Why is it such a big deal?"

That was how he had reasoned with her after she had freaked out on hearing he was twenty-eight, not twenty-one as he had first led her to believe.

"Nah! The boss had loads to drink at a lunchtime meeting. He won't even notice I'm gone. I might even head down to the skate park in a bit. Just gotta get out of this stupid suit, then I can be free again. Be *me* again!"

Erin arched her neck upwards, so her face was turned towards his. A sudden urge to kiss him had encouraged her more daring side to emerge. She placed her feet on his coffee-coloured shoes in order to reach his mouth more easily. Kieran groaned with obvious pleasure as their lips came together. It was a swooping kiss, a rollercoaster feeling. He squeezed her body closer to his, his hands cupping around her cheeks. It reminded her of an old black and white poster in her mum's office, an image of a man and woman embracing in front of the Eiffel Tower.

"Hmmm... what brought that on, girl?" Kieran grunted. There was no question that he was enjoying himself. "It's a shame we can't go somewhere more private."

His hands moved down her back.

For some reason, the way he lowered his tone and pushed his hips into her with such urgency made Erin shudder. It was like he was practising magic, conjuring extraordinary emotion and responses from her. The way he kissed her, how he smelt, and now how he looked at her with such an obvious desire. He held a power over her. She was at his mercy– and he knew it.

It was the reason she would respond in a heartbeat whenever he messaged her. And it was also why she continued to meet with him like this, despite now knowing he was so much older than her- *and* that he clearly wanted more adult things to happen between them.

And yet, when his voice and body movements transformed into the more suggestive realms, she found herself retreating from him. She knew, deep down, that it could lead her to places she would struggle to come back from.

"Shall we go for a walk? I need to go to the hospital soon, you know, to see my brother. But the skate park is in that direction, so..." Erin attempted, but Kieran had already backed away from her.

"Well, we could, but y'know, people might see us down there. And I know you don't want Daddy finding out, what with him working so close to Houses of Parliament."

His reasoning was solid, but Erin knew it was hollow in feeling. The chance that Kieran gave a damn what her dad thought about their relationship was very slim. Six feet tall and built like a machine, she knew Kieran bore no fears about an angry father hounding him down.

"Is it the skate park you don't want to go near... with me?" she dared.

Kieran stiffened.

"Erin! For God's sake, we've been through this. I don't give a damn what people think about us hanging out together. The skate park is just a bit rough, that's all. It's better for you if you stay away from it. It's kind of a lad thing. That's not why I don't wanna head down there right now. It's you getting into trouble I'm thinking about!" he bristled.

This was not the first time they had debated this subject: whose reputation they were protecting the most. It seemed a pointless differentiation to her. Surely, the *point* was that they were both out of the acceptable age difference zone, no matter whose side observed them. At least her mum had been nineteen when she had met her dad. Their age difference would have meant diddly-squat by that stage.

Just as Erin was about to reach out to him again, to offer an apology in the form of a kiss, Kieran's phone burst into life inside his trouser pocket. Without glancing at her or offering any kind of reassurance, he pulled out his phone and turned away from her, leaning as far forward as possible over the bridge railings as he muttered his words into the receiver.

After what seemed like the longest two minutes ever, he finally stepped back and faced

her. His expression was difficult to read.

"Soz, Erin. I gotta go."

"Already?"

"Yeah, it's a deal I gotta go sort out. Looks like I gotta head back to the office after all."

Without waiting for an answer from her, Kieran leaned forward, placed a finger under her chin, and pulled her face towards him. His kiss was quick, urgent, and almost reassuring—but not quite. "Next time..."

He whispered the rest of the words into her ear, and her body stiffened in reaction to what sounded like an unnerving promise.

As Erin reached the hub of the South Bank, quickly walking past the bustling crowds of tourists queuing up to experience the wonders of the London Eye, she rolled her eyes at no one in particular. When they had first arrived in the capital city last year, both she and Lyndon had been so excited by all the new tourist attractions on offer, their parents had written down a weekend schedule to ensure they didn't rush through them all at once.

It didn't take long for this enthusiasm to wear off. Like this observation wheel in front of her now! She couldn't see what all the fuss was about. They had one at Coney Island, albeit older and smaller, but still! It baffled her that people were willing to spend so much time and money on it. And today, there was even a bride and groom holding champagne glasses by the entrance, waiting to exchange their wedding vows in a capsule in the sky! All so they could say they did it *their* way, with the River Thames and Houses of Parliament as their unique backdrop.

Honestly, people! she thought.

This would make Lyndon laugh when she told him. He loved it when she shared anecdotes and observations of their new English life. But just thinking about her brother, trapped in the hospital bubble his sick body had forced him into, made her shiver, despite the scorching heat of the June sunshine.

It actually made thinking of her weird encounter with Kieran only a few minutes earlier seem insignificant, even if she still felt a rumbling of anxiety. He always did leave her feeling confused and disorientated with his strange hot and cold attitude. But she had to park this now.

This was Lyndon time; he deserved her full attention when she visited him.

At least St. Thomas's hospital was situated in a convenient location, on the other side of Westminster Bridge. And it was so close to everything she needed to access, like the tube, school and… Kieran and his favourite hangouts!

Brushing that last thought aside, Erin rounded the corner of the top of the bridge stairway and set off towards the fountain by the entrance to the hospital. She had already spotted her mum talking to someone ahead.

"Mum!" she called out. Her mum didn't seem to have heard her as she didn't turn around, but then Erin realized her voice had probably been drowned out by the chorus of giggles coming from a group of young brownie girls nearby. They were huddled around a table laden with cookies to sell.

As Erin approached them, a frizzy blonde-haired girl thrust a plate out in front of her face.

"Brownie made by a brownie!" the girl announced in a triumphant voice. Out of habit—and sympathy, as Erin remembered similar days when she had been a girl scout back home–she reached into her jean pocket to locate some loose change and threw a pound into the plastic pot the girl held out to her in her other hand.

"Thank you! All the money goes to the children's wards," the brownie girl explained.

Erin nodded at her appreciatively. "That's good. My brother is in there right now," she stated.

Forcing a polite smile in the brownie girl's direction, Erin started to walk away but was abruptly stopped in her tracks by the sound of a new voice beside her, a deep but strangely melodic voice. It was a voice that carried power and commanded attention. The way it lilted up and down too quickly between intonations, it was as though it was adhering to some new rules of communication.

"I will take five brownies. And may I commend you on your presentation," the voice said.

Instinctively, Erin held her breath before she dared to turn her head to the left to catch a look at the person behind the voice.

"You!" she gasped when she saw her.

It was unbelievable. Was it possible she was here? The girl she had seen so vividly in her dreams?

The girl turned to face her. The cloak she was wearing over her jeans and polo top—all black—swung around her ankles. It was a ridiculous costume to wear in this heat, even in a city that embraced different fashion tastes.

Erin couldn't breathe properly. Everything was wrong here: the way the strange girl stood so still, almost robotic-like, in front of her; how the dark lens on her sunglasses obscured her eyes but failed to prevent a flicker of light from illuminating behind them; and the smell that emanated from her—no longer the chocolate mint of her dreams but now a confusing mix of floral scents. It was so overwhelming. It conjured an image in Erin's mind of this black-cloaked girl twirling around the first floor of Saks Fifth Avenue's, spraying herself with every perfume tester on display!

"Yes, *me!*" the girl finally replied matter-of-factly, as though they were already acquaintances.

Erin opened her mouth to respond, but she was still struggling to catch her breath. After what seemed like an eternity—and a considerable lack of oxygen supply to Erin's body—the mysterious young woman nodded at her before turning and walking away. Erin exhaled loudly as she let her head fall down to her knees to counteract the sudden dizziness.

"Here's your cake you paid for. It might help you feel better?" the brownie girl offered, leaning over the table above her.

With a dramatic push up from both her knees, Erin bounced her upper body upright and grabbed the brownie from the girl, shovelling the entire cake into her mouth and consuming it in one hearty gulp. The brownie girl's advice *was* sound. It had been nearly eight hours since she had eaten anything, and in this stifling heat, she knew she would probably faint if she didn't get some sugar into her body.

"I think I'm going mad!" Erin whispered to herself.

The brownie girl giggled. "She did look quite cool, hey? That girl who was here just then? Like one of those catwalk models or even Katy Perry. I saw a YouTube video of Katy Perry where she was surrounded by all these cats crawling all over her. Very weird but totally cool."

"Yes, totally awesome," Erin replied.

In other circumstances, Erin would have enjoyed chatting about music videos with the brownie girl. Those were her favourite kind of conversations. But, today was different. Today, everything felt wrong. It was as though she had entered a different dimension, where emotional torture was as abundant as oxygen. First, Kieran, with his disconcerting yo-yo attitude towards her, and then this strange girl she

had been dreaming about just appearing in front of her. All of this with a sick brother she needed to visit in the building ahead of her.

She now felt sick—sick in the head!

"Hey, Erin! You're early! I thought you were going to hang out with your school friends for a bit longer?"

It was her mum, standing in front of her. The low-lying sun behind her beamed soft light out, like a halo around her head.

"Yeah, the girls went home to study," Erin replied. Instinctively, she reached her arms out to her mum, desperate for a reassuring hug from her. Stefanie started to respond, her arms extending forward, but then an urgent cry from a woman in a nurse's uniform behind them forced her mum to jerk backwards.

"Mrs. Barrett, can you come back in? Lyndon is calling for you," the nurse pleaded, shooting Erin an apologetic look.

"Go!" Erin urged her mum, quickly dropping her arms down to her side.

Without hesitation, her mum started to run back towards the hospital entrance. Back towards the child who needed her the most. Or at least this was what Stefanie Barrett assumed.

3

DIAIRES

I n the case of my death or an unfortunate incident that results in this diary being out of my hands, please:

DESTROY IT!

I'd appreciate your respect for my privacy, and I don't think that anything you read in here will please anyone. Thanks,

Stef x

THE WORDS on the torn pages jumped out at Erin, as though tiny black letters were sparking out from the unleashed paper in a bid to free themselves. The i's and t's spun around in front of her eyes in a teasing dance.

Erin had a choice to make, and it was a simple one. She could respect the wishes of the writer and close the diary. Then the words would fall back to their respective positions on the lined paper, safe from the temptation of her curious mind.

Or she could do what she had known she would do the moment she saw the book hidden in her mum's old camera case: *read it!*

It is funny how some days, you can feel as though you actually bear beauty and then others, you feel quite plain. Today has been one of my plain days. As usual, I am angry at myself and wish I had gone to school and not allowed myself so much time to think.

No surprise that it's my "wonderful" father causing me grief. He has, once again, made me feel like the worst person in the world (or at least tried to). If only he could realise that when he criticizes everyone (usually me), he is actually talking about himself! How come everyone can see that but him?

No one understands though. Everyone else's dads are really quiet or relaxed. I sometimes wish my dad could be more like Rachel's dad.

Don't get me wrong, I love my dad <u>very</u> much. I am just starting to realise you can love someone but not really like them. I've been thinking recently that my low self-esteem probably has a lot to do with my dad's attitude towards me. I know it is mainly my fault, but he doesn't get how much he hurts me, or if he does, he obviously doesn't care.

Johnny said to me, quite simply and honestly, "He's a right bastard, isn't he?"

The frightening thing is that we are his kids, so we must have inherited some of his characteristics.

Oh, well! That's just great!

S x

P.S. I had that weird dream again last night!

. . .

"OH MY GOD!" Erin heard herself shout, loud enough for Dobby to jump off her bed and ram his whole body into the wall in attempt to escape. Shaking her head at the overweight, wrinkly dog she was in charge of in her brother's absence, she got up to open her bedroom door to let him out.

Lyndon would be cross at her for forgetting his instructions to make sure doors were left open at *all times* for his beloved and now rather blind pug. Dobby had to be able to navigate at high speeds whenever the mood took him.

What kind of big sister was she? Her brother was still stuck in hospital and not looking at all good, regardless of how many times her parents tried to reassure her that his treatment was working. And she couldn't even make sure his dog was being cared for in the spirit of basic human (or dog) rights!

"Sorry, Dobby!" she shouted down the winding staircase. No response. Well, only her own echo.

This house was way too big. It was fine when it was full of people; then it made sense. It was like a modern-day version of *Downton Abbey*, with staff and guests filling up the long hallways, full of noise and purpose. But on a day like today, when it was just her and an old, blind dog, it felt more like a punishment.

Erin whistled for Dobby to come back. She needed another moving, living, real thing that she trusted near her, but she knew he wouldn't respond. One of the house masters must have put the fire on in the lounge before they left for the evening. Well, there was no chance she could compete with that.

Biting down on her lip, she turned back into the sanctuary of her bedroom, where she could close the door and put some music on to distract herself from the uncertainty of the house's creaks. Hopefully, her mum would be back from the hospital soon, and she could relax again. Erin sat down on her bed to search under her crumpled duvet for her phone but stopped when her hands found the rubbery texture

of the diary's cover instead.

Never mind what kind of sister she was; what kind of daughter was she? The teenage version of her mum had made it clear on the first page of this diary that it should not be read by anyone—under any circumstances! But even then, it was highly unlikely that the writer, this thirteen-year-old girl in 1993, could ever have imagined that her future daughter would deceive her. If she had, there was no way she would have written all this stuff down in here.

Why didn't her mum burn it? She must have been traipsing it around with her for years between all the different houses and countries she had lived in!

Erin tapped her fingers on the broken lock, which sat pointlessly at an odd angle on the front cover of the diary. She couldn't help smiling at the bizarre logo on the front cover which read: "NAF NAF". What a weird thing to call a diary. Or was it a chain? Either way, it made sense. Her mum had started saying funny northern things recently like, "It's a bit naff," or Erin's personal favourite: "What a numpty!"

Her mum's northern English roots had always seemed so remote before they had moved to the UK. In America, everyone just assumed her mum was the posh English wife of a diplomat. But since they moved to London, the first thing people said on meeting her was: "Oh, you haven't lost your northern accent, then!"

It's funny though, the fact that her mum used to live in the North of England and was once a teenager too. This had never really occurred to her before now. Well, not properly anyway. She'd never thought about her parents being kids or teenagers or having had troubles and worries.

The fact that her mum's parents had divorced when Stefanie was a teenager had never been discussed in great detail—something about it all being too difficult to keep re-living. And Erin knew her dad had suffered a lot as a kid too. Adam was brought up in foster homes and never met his mum or even knew who his dad was. But these were just the historic credentials of the people who had brought her into the world. It was just who they were: Stefanie and Adam Barrett, her parents.

But now Erin had this diary, it was like she had found a secret portal. It was a way into her mum's world, the one she must have inhabited before her dad came along and took her under his wing and, well, basically saved her from what seemed like a lot of chaos!

There was no doubt about it. By reading secrets of her mum's youth, Erin would be opening a door she probably shouldn't. But it was too late. She had stepped inside, and now she had no intention of going back out again until she had found some answers.

And jeez, did she need some of those right now. The mysterious diamond-eyed girl had come to her during her sleep again last night, this time in a less dramatic scene. She was standing in a pool of water with others who looked just like her whilst coloured mist swirled around them. It wasn't threatening this time. It was just unnerving for a reason she couldn't quite place and left her feeling confused about the message she was supposed to take from it.

Perhaps it wasn't so wrong of her to try to understand the most important person in her life or to see if she had any clearer messages to share. Yes, this book was a container of dark secrets, but it was already revealing crucial answers. Her mum had been on emotional speedway before Erin had been welcomed into the world. And the teenage Stefanie had referred to *that* dream! Was it *possible* that it was similar to hers? Well, there was only one way to find out!

Erin picked up the diary again. Holding it under her nose, she flicked her thumb over the pages as if preparing to shuffle a deck of cards. She breathed in the waft of musky air it released between the thin sheaths of paper. It was an instinctive reaction, this sudden urge to breathe in the scent of her mum's history and to feel the vibrations of her journey. She wanted to know everything—even the bad stuff that was bound to be in there. Maybe even references to any dreams the younger Stefanie had experienced back then?

"Okay, Mum. I'm sorry, but I'm just gonna go ahead and read this thing you really should have destroyed yourself."

Jeez, am I actually talking out loud now?

Erin shook her head and giggled self-consciously at herself.

Searching for her phone again, she finally found it under her pillow.

On cue, a message popped up on the phone screen.

Kieran is typing...

Yes! Her heart jolted in response to the promise that the words on her phone screen had just delivered. Kieran was writing to her at last! Or at least he was teasing her, filling her with false hope that they would exchange some form of contact today. She had a strong suspicion this uncertainty was all part of his game, a way for him to keep control of their communication with each other.

Sometimes a message *would* actually come through—a random photo of some street art he liked or a video of his latest skater flip. Stupidly, she always re-played his videos too. This was mainly to feed his ego because she knew that's what he really wanted. And then she would receive her reward: another photo or video message from him.

Or, if she was really lucky, he would bother to send her actual words. These were the messages she most longed for. They helped her determine if he was sending words meant just for her and not a hundred other girls on his list.

But quite often, the promise would not deliver; no message would come through. Then she would be left in a state of manic phone-checking limbo. It drained her of all energy and enthusiasm for all the things she used to love doing before he came into her life. It felt like an internal light she could only turn on again when he bothered to flip the switch.

"Send me a message or don't bother at all. Make your mind up, goddammit!" Erin growled at her phone, throwing it at her bedroom wall in frustration. The phone landed just short of the door frame, narrowly missing Dobby, who had made a tentative return to her room. He darted away again in the face of another Erin outburst.

"Sorry, Dobby!" Erin mumbled an apology whilst picking up her mum's diary in search of salvation. She flicked the pages to somewhere in the middle of 1995. She knew her mum would have been about fifteen then—the same age she was now.

MAY 21, 1995

I can't believe what happened this weekend. My dad would go crazy if he knew, but it could have been a lot worse.

The party was in a massive field at the back of the Mayfield's farm. We very nearly didn't bother going because we all assumed it would be a lot of church singing and kumbaya by the campfire—which I actually don't mind normally. But Rachel had managed to get some of that 20/20 drink from the local offie (she always gets served when she gets her boobs out in one of those crop tops she wears), and we fancied letting our hair down. I think Rachel was relieved I'd finally lightened up and stopped being such a "God Botherer", as she called me. We had a massive fall-out about it, but I've let it go now. I know she is just teasing me and wants me to have fun and chill out.

But anyway, the party was NOT a churchy sing-along at all! The whole setup was brilliant. There were tree trunks all around a huge bonfire, with a CD player in the background playing my kind of music—Aerosmith and Bon Jovi and none of that pop crap that they always think we want at the school discos. It all felt so cool, like a scene from an American movie that I had always wanted to be in.

Everyone was drinking! And you couldn't really see people that well when you talked to them, which made the whole thing kind of mysterious. It was like we were being a bit hedonistic (I like that word), and the 20/20 stuff mixed with some of that white cider went right to my head!

Anyway, a few of us were just chilling, and as we chatted, this boy (well, MAN. I thought he was about nineteen or something, but he is thirty!) came over to talk to me. I have never met anyone like him before. Everyone else was dancing and smoking or getting off with each other, and he just came over and said, "Lie back with me."

I laughed at first, thinking he was dodgy. But he had this little torch with him, and he shone it under my chin and whispered, "I saw you when you first joined the party, before it got so dark, and I was seriously drawn to you. I clocked you straightaway. You've got those big, brown eyes, like Beth from Neighbours.*"*

And then he took my hand and laid down on the grass. He pointed up at the star-lit sky and just started talking to me about the stars

and the universe and how we are all made of star stuff. He kind of blew my mind. He knew all this stuff that I hadn't really thought about before, like I had been trapped in some bubble of ignorance about life and where we come from. I've been going to church every week and singing about God and Jesus and then this guy—his name is Warren—comes along and just knocks me off my feet.

I could see Rachel rolling her eyes at me across the bonfire because she knows I'm such a romantic. But it just made me feel so alive hearing Warren talk like this. And even when he kind of ruined it by singing "Babe" by Take That into my ear, I still couldn't resist him, and yes... I went with him.

I know he wanted a lot more than kissing. He kept moving his hips into my mine and rubbing against me, but he didn't touch me anywhere else. He did say (too loudly for my liking) that he wanted to make love to me all night, but he couldn't because I was only fifteen!

Rachel heard him say that, marched over to grab my hand, and announced that we had to get home—thank God for Rachel! No way would I ever want to do that! I found out later that Warren was married but getting a divorce and then it hit me. Like, why would a thirty-year-old be messing about in a field and singing cheesy Take That songs to a schoolgirl?

I was totally born in the wrong times. I should be wearing long, flowing dresses held in by corsets and going to afternoon garden parties like Scarlett O'Hara—a time when the men had to work hard just to get a dance out of a girl, never mind feeding cheesy compliments to get a lay with under-age girls!

Guess some things are best as fantasies—beats the reality of

growing up in the sex-mad nineties!

Love, S x

P.S. Yeah, I had that weird dream again, by the way!

Erin jumped up off her bed and spun herself around in the middle of her room. The diary was clutched to her chest as she made that shriek reserved for the extremely squeamish occasions.

"Oh my God, Mum!" she said out loud.

Running over to her mirror, she confirmed the colour of her reflection matched the burning in her cheeks. The orange freckles on her pale complexion always looked more pronounced when accompanied by a fierce, red blush. Erin looked so like her dad when she was embarrassed. The redness of her hair and skin was such a contrast to her mum's olive skin and honey brown hair, which Lyndon had so unfairly inherited. But she did have big, brown eyes like her mum. She made a mental note to look up the character Beth from this TV programme *Neighbours*, so she could see what kind of compliments her mum had been buttered up with by this older guy.

Honestly, the parallel between 1995 Mum and what she herself was going through now was unbelievable: an older guy wanting a bit more. It was just her situation now, with Kieran—*and* the weird dream reference again!

Erin so wanted to talk to her mum about this. She wanted to reach out to her and ask her for some help to fix this mess she was in. Or that her stupid heart was in, anyway. But how could she ask her mum any of this when they had never had *those* kinds of conversations?

And she certainly couldn't tell her that she thought they might have shared similar teenage situations. Then she would have to admit she had been reading her mother's diary!

But more than anything, she really couldn't expect her mum to listen to this stuff when her other child was in hospital, fighting for his life! There was no contest between her needs and her brother's right now. They both had parts of themselves that were hungry for some of their mother's healing love, but Lyndon's need was the greater, by far. She was on her own with this one—or maybe not quite?

There *was* someone locked back in time who might be able to understand what she was going through, even if she couldn't talk back to her. As crazy as it sounded, even in her own head, she couldn't help playing with an impossible idea, one that involved trying to find some connection with her mum through the threads of time, an invisible loom that would somehow tie their thoughts and experiences together.

Way too much sci-fi nonsense, Erin! Isn't it enough you have some weird dream ability going on? Now you're thinking time travel communication too! she scolded herself.

But still, she reached over to her desk and pulled out a notebook from the bottom of the pile of school books she was so determined to ignore. It was a plain purple notebook with three names printed on the cover in silver: Erin Mae Barrett. An empty lined notebook waiting to be filled with the thoughts and dreams of the person whose name dominated the front. The book was a Christmas stocking present from last year—their last one in Washington before the big move over here.

She had discarded it as a bit lame at the time, yet another attempt by her mum to turn her into a "creative" person like she was—someone who wrote down their feelings.

But she now understood why her mum had given it to her. This was a gift that really could keep on giving. What could be more healing than taking control of her own thoughts and giving them the freedom to come alive on paper? And then keeping them protected from the rest of the world? What a way to express herself, to work out what was going on in her head without the fear of it being copied, shared, re-tweeted, or mocked by someone else in the abyss of cyberspace.

And best of all, what better way for her to find a connection to her mum, even if it would be a one-sided exchange?

She opened the book and began to write.

JUNE 16, 2015

Dear Stefomum (my diary name for you),

I READ YOUR DIARY TODAY. I'm sorry. I know you made it clear no one should read it, but hopefully, you will understand as we go along this journey together. I want to share stuff with you right now, in 2015, but I just can't for so many reasons. So, I'm going to write to you in 1995 instead.

Anyway, it seems that you and I are living parallel lives; me in 2015 and you in 1995. I wonder if we would have been friends, if I were there or you were here? I like to think we would have. You sound like the kind of girl I would want to be friends with, although maybe a bit crazy romantic with all your meanderings!

And by the way, I do love how you phrased "went with this guy". I thought it meant something a lot bigger than that when I first read it, but then I realised it was really quite innocent kissing you kept referring to. I know Dad was your first—you waited for the right one, etc. (At least I hope that is true after you made such a big deal out of it to me. I guess I will find out if I keep on reading!)

But I do like the way you handle yourself with guys—the way you keep saying "I'm not that bothered... he gave me his number, but I didn't call him... it wasn't going anywhere..."

Hilarious, Stefomum! How would you have coped with being fifteen in 2015, I wonder? You CAN'T avoid anyone in my timeline anymore. It's almost impossible to move on from anyone or any interaction (however innocent) because they never really go away! Once you have made a connection with them, once they know your name and can track you down on one of your profiles, that's it! You are forever in the periphery of their thoughts, and you in theirs. Trust me, it's exhausting!

Can I even describe it to you, the way we live now, in a world where we get up and operate like robots who are obsessed with and controlled by our little machines? We have devices that we stupidly fill with crazy apps that rule our lives and connect us to all these networks we form with people we can't even remember meeting or wish we never had!

If you had met that older guy in 2015, Stefomum, he would be following you on Twitter, Facebook, Snapchat and Instagram, and you wouldn't even know about it! You wouldn't have the luxury of saying, "It wasn't going anywhere," because you wouldn't be in control of it. That one kiss you shared with some older, married guy (divorced or not) would have been caught on a phone, saved, shared and stored as ammunition against you without you even realizing it. You would have been tongue-tied with him forever by the power of the internet! Take that, 1995!

I read this article the other day claiming that my generation lives in an uber-connected world: "Technology has revolutionized the

world and made us one big, global family". But you know what? That's just crap, Stefomum. You guys had it way better.

We are more disconnected than ever. No one needs to go outside or travel anymore to make a connection because the machines do it for us! And every time you make a new connection with someone, it's like you've taken one more step towards overload. You've got so many choices, so many connections that you end up just feeling like pulling the plug on the whole lot. It makes my head hurt!

I wish I could share this with you now, Stefomum. I kind of feel like I'm sinking... or falling... and I'm not really sure which. Either way, it feels pretty lonely.

It's like there's no one around me anymore to pull me out or to catch me if I fall. I can't seem to find a lifeboat or a safety net anymore. When did that happen to me... to us... our family?

It didn't used to be like this. I always felt secure in our family nest. We all did, didn't we? We used to be so close, only a couple of years ago, before London, before Lyndon got so sick...

Ping! Erin's phone lit up from where it still lay on the floor, sounding out at her for attention. She jumped up in automatic response, her reflexes reacting to her device in the same way they would shiver in response to a sudden blast of cold air.

It could be him! Kieran's message could have finally come through.

She glanced at the screen.

Candy Crush Saga: Mia Jones sent you a request.

Another Facebook update! Where was he? She was back to square one again, alerted and deflated all at once. The loneliness was palpable. Once again, she was stranded in a silent house, with only a ping to invite her to reconnect with the outside world.

It was moral question time again. *Do you do the right thing, Erin? Ring Mum and see how Lyndon is? Find out if you should make a start on dinner? Or do you do the wrong thing—but the one you know will make you feel better—and go to him?*

She clicked on her photo library and sent a selfie to Kieran alongside the caption: *"I guess the mountain had better come to you."*

4

DOORS

Erin's failure to deliver on her promise to invite Serenity and Liberty back to her house had long since passed its excuse deadline. It was time to bite the bullet and let them into her world for a couple of hours. What could she lose? Even if it was obvious these girls were only interested in seeing what kind of "palace" she lived in.

Erin's instincts never failed her about these kinds of things. From the moment news had broken in school that Erin was *that* Barrett—the daughter of the ambassador with the coolest house ever—the shallow motivations of her schoolmates had become blindingly clear. Her chances of finding a genuine comrade in arms had depleted to zero. At least by keeping the social media vultures close by, she could secure herself some protection—*and* some inside knowledge.

Kieran's messages were getting more intense by the day. A crash course in game-playing skills had become essential. It was like she was drowning in the dramatic, un-chartered waters he had created around her. Somehow, he had thrown her into a paradoxical ocean of emotion, where dolphins leaped over the moonlit vista in one direction, but then sharks jumped out at her in the other. It was like living permanently on edge, waiting to see which direction he would send her in next.

If there was any chance of holding her head up high, of even breathing properly again, she needed to know how to keep herself afloat. And these alpha girls were the experts in social survival.

Snapchat from Kieran

Perfect timing! Erin thought. *Let's see what he has to say today.* Maybe she could sound out the girls for some clever, power-

regaining responses? She clicked on the blue square to see what mood he was in.

Hey, Barry. How you doing, hun?

Okay, so far, so good. Even if Kieran was sticking with the weird habit of calling her boyish names derived from her surname. He had told her it was something to do with his Army background, apparently. All the guys called each other versions of their surnames. He had friends with names like Boggy, Dinga, and even Swampy! And so, naturally, she was Barry! It didn't *really* bother her. At least it showed some thought had been put into what he was messaging to her.

More importantly, it showed this was not a generic message he had sent to all the other girls she suspected he played around with. She quickly replied.

I'm good, thanks! I finished my last exam today.

Oh, God, why did she mention her exam? Another clumsy confirmation of how young she was in comparison to him!

Kieran had messaged back already.

Hmm... are you still wearing that cute school uniform? Photo for me?

Erin checked to see the girls were safely absorbed in the light from their own hand-held machines before creeping over to the bathroom at the side of the den. Careful to ensure the door was firmly closed, she quickly fumbled with her shirt buttons, undoing just enough of them to allow a glimpse of cleavage, and then took a quick photo of her reflection in the mirror. Frantically, she sent it back to him as quickly as she could.

This was the sort of thing she had always sworn to avoid, but a quick response to him was vital if she were to keep the communication line open. He would probably be heading over to the skate park soon, so her online time with him could be limited.

The photo worked. His message flashed up instantly.

Oh my God, Harry! You look so damn cute in that photo. Pigtails next time?

It was *Harry* now, was it?

Still feeling the need to rush, she quickly pulled two hair bands from her wrist, split her hair into a middle parting, and tied it into two high bunches on either side of her face. Within seconds, she had taken another snap in the mirror, quickly filtered it to black and white to hide the blush she knew was now visible, and then sent it to him without stopping to consider the potential outcome. It was a race against time.

A red box flashed up by his name. A photo back from him! Excellent! She clicked on it immediately and then nearly dropped her phone in the toilet basin, shocked.

What was he thinking?

Her heart pounded in her chest as she picked the phone up from where it had fallen on the floor. The image had already disappeared. He had only allocated her a ten-second viewing time, but it was enough.

Erin bit down on her lip and swallowed hard, not sure how to respond. Her immediate thought was to ask him to send her the photo again. That way, she could show it to the girls and see how they reacted. Not a good idea. They *would* be impressed. But she knew they would tell her to send him a revealing photo back! And then it would just get back to everyone at school! Now *that* would be a mistake. Everyone would want to know more about this older guy who was sending photos of himself in full morning glory. A recipe for disaster! She had to keep this one to herself.

"Where are the snacks you promised?" she heard Liberty call out to her.

Erin ignored her and made a snap decision. This time, *she* would be the one to end the conversation; see how he liked it! As quietly as possible, she sneaked out of the bathroom and ran upstairs to her bedroom, where a myriad of teddies and dolls sat assembled together on a rocking chair in the corner of the room. They had been on too many journeys across the world with her; relegating them to the cupboard didn't seem right.

Without pausing to think it through, she picked up a pink Care Bear and positioned it next to her cheek, then pulled her best shocked— but hopefully cute—expression. A quick snap and a press of a button and the image disappeared into Kieran's message stream, along with the caption:

This schoolgirl is so shocked, she is regressing! Lol!

And then followed up with another message:

Made me smile (and blush though). Catch ya later, Larry x

As always, staring at the screen, waiting for the symbol next to his name to change, didn't speed anything up. Once again, she was frozen in a trance-like state, lingering to see how—or if—he would respond.

At last, the symbol changed, an indication that he had opened the messages. Five minutes passed. No reply.

And there it was again. That familiar, sinking feeling of remorse rushing through her entire body, like an avalanche of self-esteem crashing down. It was no use trying to regain some control in this game. He always had the upper hand. Any small moment of victory she had felt by trying to take back some power just left her feeling empty again. She regretted signing with a kiss already. It gave him too much!

"*Or* not enough!" she reasoned to the Care Bear she still held in her hand. "Shit! Why did you start this, Kieran?" she growled at the phone in her other hand.

Throwing the teddy down, she pressed the icon on the top right of her phone camera screen to switch it to selfie mode, pulled down her skirt and panties, and took the photo she knew he was so desperate for her to send him. It made her feel sick just looking at the image, even when filtered to a neutral black and white. Hadn't she always sworn she would never do such a stupid thing like this?

Never give yourself away. Once an image is out there, you can never really take it back.

How many times had her dad warned her of this? And how many times had she chucked a cushion at him? Begged him to stop telling her things she knew already?

Her finger hovered over the send button on the screen. Just one touch. That is all it would take for the image to reach Kieran. But then what? Yes, it would generate a quicker response than a stupid teddy bear photo, but at what cost?

Almost laughing at herself and at how near she had come to losing all sense, she clicked away from Kieran's message feed and threw the phone on the floor. It landed in an upright position, just in front of the Care Bear, and in such a way that it looked like the teddy was holding it in its lap.

"That was close!" she shuddered.

She lay back on her bed in a defeated heap, then rolled onto her front to pull out the purple notebook from where it was digging into her, concealed by a mountain of clothes she had recently taken to sleeping amongst. The enthusiasm she had felt about her new huge walk-in wardrobe when they had first moved in had already vanished.

Opening the notebook, she scanned the pages now filled with her recently scribbled vents. This writing lark really was cathartic. It was perfect for ridding her body of the poisonous thoughts that threatened to make her sick if she didn't get it all out. It was like she had broken a seal to her emotions. Once she had started, she couldn't stop. It was a sure-fire way to release some of the anguish, excitement, and confusion that permanently bubbled inside of her, a cauldron of her mixed-up secrets!

The vacuous girls in the den were of no use to her. They would freak

if they knew she had sent a photo of her teddy as a response to Kieran's photo of himself. She could hear them taunting her now: *"What kind of loser does that?"*

But she knew someone who would understand. Someone whose views she cared a lot more about too.

JUNE 29, 2015

DEAR STEFOMUM,

The man I told you about before—the older one—he is messing me up! I can't seem to switch off whatever it is that he has turned on within me. How is that? How can another person have the power to turn you on or off? Did this happen to you too?

It looks like you did have a guy who tried to play you. You wrote about him, the one you said looked like David Beckham. I could feel your pain when I read your words about how he made you feel so foolish. How he gave you a piece of paper from his pocket for you to wrap up your finished chewing gum, and you saw it was a receipt for condoms— clearly not meant for you!

I actually threw your diary down on the floor in frustration at you when I read that. How did you stop yourself from hitting him when he said, "Oh, yeah, you buy twelve and get three free... I've got four left." What a dick! Excuse the language, Stefomum, but honestly, I would have kicked him, for sure! This is where a bit of our 2015 approach would have been very useful! You could have bombarded every one of his social media platforms with that story! Put him right in his place.

I doubt that would have been your style though. You've never been a revenge-seeker. You've always told me and Lyndon to be on good terms with all people wherever possible. Don't hold grudges.

But you stood your ground, and you didn't give in to him. You knew he was just a silly boy with a gigantic ego (just because he looked like some famous curtain-haired footballer—so what?) and clearly was not worthy of you. You weren't in love with him. I bet sending both him and his condoms to use with some other stupid girl was a no-brainer for you.

But that's my problem with Kieran. He isn't a silly boy. He's a man, and... I'm pretty sure that I'm in love with him!

And I think—well, sorry, I KNOW he is getting impatient with the physical side of things. He sent me a YouTube clip (a music video clip) the other day. He does that sometimes—shares a favourite song or a lyric. He says he finds it easier to tell me how he feels through music because it's hard for guys to talk about their feelings. You even asked me why I was suddenly listening to Stereophonics and Radiohead the other day.

(That is, you as in when you are thirty-five... now in 2015... as my grown-up mum! This is so weird!)

But the last few music clips have been more obvious. I thought he was just trying to wind me up at first. He sent me this song called "Blurred Lines", which he knows I hate because I told him Dad once tried to mimic the dance after a few beers in the kitchen and ended up putting his back out! You were NOT impressed, by the way!

But the next two songs he sent to me were more direct, making it clear what he wants to happen between us—and sooner, rather than later. I don't think there are any blurred lines about the meaning of songs with titles like "You Shook Me All Night Long", or even worse, "I Want To Be Your Underwear" (you'll get to hear this next year when it is released in 1996—lucky you!)"

I felt like writing back, "Yeah, sure, be my underwear. You can use the pad I'm wearing as a pillow!"

I know, I know, that would have been a VERY embarrassing and stupid thing to say to him. I guess it's my feminist side coming out, or more likely, the fact that I don't know what to do when he brings up that elephant in the room!

He is such a Jekyll and Hyde though, and it is so confusing.

The last time I saw him, it was like a movie. He left me breathless – and confused! We didn't have long to meet. You told me I could meet with some new school friends before meeting you at the hospital. I didn't though —sorry!

I met him on the Millennium Bridge (not even built in your time yet!) after he'd finished work. I was surprised he wanted to meet me there as it's so busy. He kissed me like he couldn't get enough of me! I honestly thought to myself, this is it... this is what happiness is! This is what it feels like to be in love!

If I could have pressed a pause button on that moment and somehow bottled that feeling, I honestly think I could feed off the energy he gave me for the rest of my life!

But here's the thing, Stefomum. I realise now that moments don't get stalled, paused, or frozen. They move forward and pull us on to the next stage. That high I was on with him in that moment... he was never going to let me stay up there for too long. As soon as I pulled away from him, he *whispered in my ear words that sent me plummeting down in one big crash. Words that broke me right out of his spell.*

"You know that next time we see each other, we will sleep together, don't you?"

I didn't respond because I didn't know what to say. He didn't message me back for FIVE days!

He's like a puppet master! He makes me dance to his seductive tune and then leaves me hanging, right arm, left leg, disembodied and immobilized in a heart-wrenching, mid-air suspension with no warning when the music will resume again!

Erin jumped up from her bed, notebook in one hand and phone in the other. The girls in her den had long been forgotten. Her last paragraph had given her an idea.

So, Kieran liked to give her funny boy names? Well, she would give him a nickname too: Master of Puppets (M.O.P). She also knew where she could find the framed album cover that James Hetfield had signed for her dad on Metallica's last tour. She would take a photo of that and send it to Kieran later on when the silence between them became too unbearable, as it so often did.

If this was the day he had chosen to send her pictures of himself without his pants on, then fine! And if it was a bit of teasing he was after, then she could play this game too. But *her* strategy would NOT be to give him what he so wanted so easily.

Erin smiled to herself as she tucked her notebook under her pillow and made her way down the stairs, towards the kitchen, where she knew the M.O.P. frame was hanging. She was just about to push the door open and barge in but stopped herself at the last minute.

Something was very wrong. She could feel it... an instinct... her guardian angel... who knew what? It told her with every ounce of her being NOT to open the door. She didn't. Instead, she took three steps back and stared at the door. She was eerily aware of her frantic heart pounding in her ears, mixed with the frightening sound of both her parents' anguished voices in a heated conversation with someone else. There was a man's voice, one she did not recognise. His voice was deep and gravelly. It gave him authority and made her feel utterly terrified for reasons she could not identify. She listened from the other side of the door.

Every part of her body screamed at her to walk away, yet she couldn't move. Sheer terror had immobilised her. A sudden hissing sound vibrated around the edges of the wooden door frame separating her from whatever strangeness was occurring inside the kitchen. A purple mist slowly seeped out around the side of the hinges, dancing in a swirling rhythm before it was sucked back in again. It reminded her of the coloured mists that swirled around the diamond-eyed people in her dreams.

Erin felt bile rise in her throat and fill her mouth as she reached her arm out to the banister of the staircase to steady herself. She wanted to scream out for her mum, to feel the sanctity of her dad's arms around her. Something, a primeval instinctive feeling, told her that *someone* was threatening her family lifeline, and there was nothing she could do about it.

Calm down, for God's sake, Erin! It's probably just some crazy CIA experiment Dad is involved in these days!

She scolded herself, almost laughing out loud at how absurd her paranoia was.

But then, why would her mum be in the room too?

It didn't add up. She knew she should walk away. The Master of Puppets photo could wait. Whatever was going on in the kitchen conjured much more threatening images in her mind than the one Kieran had sent her earlier. A strategy to deal with *his* games could be dealt with later. Right now, there was something much more mysterious pulling her towards it.

Yet, despite being the one to always scream at the TV, *"Who the hell opens the door when it is obvious the madman is behind it?"* she knew she would have to keep to script.

She just had to take a quick peek.

Erin walked over to the slight opening in the door, taking care to avoid making any sound as the soles of her sandals gently pressed down on the wooden floor, and carefully rested her forehead to the door frame.

It was worse than she could have imagined. Her mum and dad were sitting close to each other, their hands both gripping the sides of their chairs. They stared up at a huge, dome-shaped hovering cinema screen that expanded across the width and ceiling of the room. It was like a sadistic planetarium had been set up in the kitchen. But instead of stars and wonder, it was a universe of coloured mist swirling around the looming, distorted face of one man—a godlike figure who was booming out words that terrified her mum and angered her dad.

Erin held her breath, moved her fingers over the button at the top of her phone to click it into silence, and leaned closer to hear what this terrifying presence was saying. He was clearly looking at her mum.

"There is a lot of energy within you, Mrs. Barrett. I can see why you were suggested as a suitable candidate, and I can assure you that I can grant you the health miracle you need for your son. But as I said, I do expect this to be an exchange. So, in order for us to make the arrangements for your son's treatment, we will need you to confirm your agreement to this exchange with my agents by tomorrow morning at the latest. Is this understood?"

Erin put her hand to her mouth to stop herself from making the noise she wanted to make. *Dad!* she screamed inside. *What is going on? What are they going to do to Mum?*

But she remained quiet and waited, silently willing her dad to tell this creature—or whatever it was—to go to hell. But instead, the man she had adored for as long as she could remember, her protector, her everything, responded in a brisk, curt tone with, "We will have an answer for you by tonight."

That was *not* what she had expected her dad to say. How could they even *contemplate* this proposal? What did this mean... an *exchange*? They wanted her mum to give them her *energy* to save Lyndon? Yeah, right, she could imagine what that meant! At least when Kieran spoke to her about wanting sex, he didn't mix it up with hidden terminology!

She may only be fifteen, but she could recognise blatant exploitation when it was staring her in the face! How could her parents not see this? How could her dad, of all people, even contemplate this craziness?

Her phone vibrated in her hand to alert her to an incoming message.

It was from Liberty.

Hey, where are you? Are you bringing those Doritos or what? We don't know our way around this mansion of yours. L x

The girls! *Damn!* She had forgotten about them. If they saw this mad, alien-like scene in her house, it would be a total catastrophe. She quickly typed back.

Soz! Stay where u r. Be down ASAP. Best go out for pizza. My dad has a VIP meeting. Top-secret shit (grimace face) My treat! E x

Erin had seen and heard enough. Taking a deep breath, she walked away from the crippling disappointment of her parents' weakness. This changed everything. The moral framework that had been so carefully laid out for her all these years was clearly built on a load of crap.

"The dreams were real," she whispered as she reached the top of the stairs. The terrifying man on the screen may have had normal-looking eyes, but all that coloured mist swirling around him was exactly like her dream visions. He had even been wearing a big, gold collared neckpiece with a purple diamond set inside an eye-shaped pendant, just like the girl in her dreams wore.

So, it *had* been a warning after all. Something worse had been lurking around the corner for them all along. It didn't matter that it involved a promise to save her brother because at what cost? Lyndon would never agree to their mum being subjected to something like this, even it did save his life. And anyway, the doctors had been sounding more positive recently. What was wrong with putting his life in the hands of trained medical experts? It had to be preferable to entering into some obscure agreement with some aliens, or whatever they were.

And then there was the appearance of the dream girl to consider, the one she had seen outside the hospital. She had to be part of this somehow. There were too many omens here to ignore the connections.

For some reason, irrational as it was, Erin had a sudden urge to do something stupid, to rebel in the face of such absurdity. If her parents felt justified to break their moral codes, then so could she!

Stopping at the top of the stairs to the den, Erin quickly opened the photo library on her phone and sent the message to Kieran she had sworn she never would:

Here you go! Think this is the photo you were really hoping for! E xx

5

GAMES

They always did this. It was their *thing:* the staring game. Lyndon always won. His in-built composure gave him a firm advantage every time. Erin was more impatient. Her body would start shaking with convulsions even before the sound of spluttering laughter left her mouth.

It had started as a means of enduring long car journeys when they were younger. Their dad had always been a stickler about children not being reliant on machines for travel entertainment. More recently, though, the game had become a necessity, a means of distraction from the disturbing orchestra of shouting and banging doors that their parents had organised between them ever since the news of Lyndon's illness had reached them. But this was a first for them—using the staring games to actually *stop* each other from laughing!

Erin held her breath and clenched her fists as she focused her eyes on the dark circles of her brother's pupils. How had it taken her so long to work out that the key was to stare into the black? Typical, then, that it was Lyndon who looked like he was going to buckle this time. And for once, she didn't want him to!

"Shh..." she whispered to him.

1... 2... 3... 4... 5...

She counted in her head as she waited for the sound of the door to Lyndon's private room to close shut. Click! *Finally*! Mariola, Lyndon's

nurse, had gone.

Their pent-up laughter erupted at exactly the same time, their differently pitched sounds pouring over each other. Erin let her head fall into the soft wrinkles of her brother's blankets, which covered his legs.

"That was the best one yet!" Lyndon spluttered between raspy coughing and the welcoming sound of his bird-squawking laughter.

"Chicken bubbles!" Erin exclaimed, choking on her words as she slapped her hands down on the hard mattress of Lyndon's hospital bed.

"I know!" Lyndon responded in between a painful-sounding coughing fit. "She is definitely my favourite nurse in here. I know Mum goes mad if she thinks we are making fun of people getting expressions wrong, but Mariola is just *so* funny. I mean... chicken bubbles? That was just pure, utter genius!"

Lyndon grinned at his sister, clearly delighted that she was at his hospital bedside just at the perfect time for his Polish nurse to have delivered one of her endearing language blunders.

Erin nodded at her brother in amiable agreement. "What did you show her on your phone to make her say such a random thing?" she asked him, letting her arm rest on the tightly pinned sheets by Lyndon's skinny legs.

"I just showed her some photos that Mum had taken of me with the Golden Retriever. Y'know, the healing dog they bring in here sometimes. It was so cute, Erin. You would've loved him. Not as cute as Dobby, of course, but still... Anyway, Mariola took one look at the photos and started welling up, saying, 'Stefanie's photos give me chicken bubbles all over!'" Lyndon started laughing again. "I mean, I

knew she *meant* goose bumps, but I can't help it. I laugh every time she comes in the room now. I'm not sure she likes it either... Oops!" Lyndon shrugged his shoulders, still grinning.

Erin stretched her arms up into the air, her mouth wide open and distorted as her smile transformed into an exhausted yawn. She hadn't slept a wink since last night, when she had heard the "mad" proposal in the family kitchen.

It felt good, being near her only sibling today. It beat being scared of what he looked like or what the wires coming in and out of his body represented: a warning of disaster, a promise of grief. Right now, all she saw when she looked at Lyndon was her ally, her comrade in arms, the only other person in the world who was as closely tied in with whatever this family mess was—even if he wasn't aware of it yet.

"Don't worry," Erin reassured him. "I reckon being a sick kid gets you let off quite a lot."

Leaning forward to the food tray table that Mariola had wheeled in between them so that they could play chess, Erin moved one of the wooden pawns on the board without even checking to see if it was a good move. Chess was another game that Lyndon always won.

Lyndon sucked in his breath loudly and made a clucking noise at his sister.

"Erin! You keep making the same mistakes over again." *You make me want to make mistakes...*

Just like that song, the one Kieran had written about her. He had sworn to her that he would record it and send it to her—another promise he had yet to fulfill. But still, she had committed the words to her memory. She relished the tragic, almost paradoxical love story the lyrics suggested.

Let's do the things your parents would hate 'cause babe, it's going to happen soon. Just you wait.

Life is too short, and soon you will see that I'm here, and I'm waiting for you to make that mistake, to finally take the bait.

Yes, I am falling, and so are you.

You think I won't catch you, but babe, you know deep down that I will!

How many nights had she fallen asleep whilst repeating those words in her head, trying to decide what he was meaning to tell her? Too many, it seemed. The words had embedded themselves into her psyche. Even in her daydreams, no matter how much she tried to push positive thoughts into her brain, she would always end up falling somehow.

It was madness, this obsession she was developing about whatever was going on between her and Kieran. He was everywhere she went; his words impregnated her thoughts and disorientated her sense of direction. Even a simple physics class had been disturbed by his oppressive influence over her. It had just been a simple lesson about the reaction of electrons to new energy sources.

If she had been a normal, stable individual, she would have done as she was instructed and copied the notes on the whiteboard. But no, she had to be reckless. She had to let her messed-up brain direct her to write a crazy, *"Erin is an electron reacting to Kieran"* version of events.

REACTION

Before you,
I was in the dark,
a tiny speck
orbiting around the hub.
And then you arrived,
a new energy,

a new light.
I reacted.
You made me jump.
I moved out of orbit.
I had no choice.
It was my reaction to you—
the one I was born to have.
I was excited;
I was out of control.
I went into a different state of being.
I lit up!
And then you left.
You took your light away.
It made me unstable.

You took me too far up.

I had no choice.
It was my reaction to you—
the one I was born to have.
There was only one place I could go.
I had to fall back...

Mr. Smith, total bastard physics teacher that he was, had chosen to pick up her book and read the entire poem out to the whole class. People were still sniggering at her when she walked past them in the school corridors. She was *still* seeing stupid photos with the hashtag "REACTION" on everyone's profiles. God! If only she could find a way to extract the memory of that nightmare from all their brains!

She thought about telling Lyndon what had happened. He was a good listener for a thirteen-year-old boy. But then, why would he want to hear about a school embarrassment drama when he was battling some form of cancer that no one could fully diagnose?

"Who's the guy, then?" Lyndon asked quietly. "The one who's making you check your phone every two minutes?"

Shit!

"No one, Lynds... just some boy at school playing games, that's all. Sorry. Let's play on." Erin budged her chair nearer to Lyndon's bed, chucking her phone, with all its Kieran-connected temptations, in the bag behind her.

Lyndon looked at her and shook his head. He pushed the food tray table away from them and sat up straighter in his bed, unable to hide his discomfort as he did.

"You get a lot of time in a hospital bed watching crazy reality shows, y'know. I reckon I've worked out quite a lot about what's going on out there from this bed. You wanna know my theory?" he asked, not waiting for Erin to answer before continuing. "It's one big game, and we're all players. We just don't know it! That's why you should probably get better at chess, Erin. It's got to be the best way to survive the times. I reckon we're *all* part of one humongous experiment. Like, *everyone* is. They just don't know it. So, imagine that every app we use is just another stage to mess with our minds! Make us more zombified, so we get distracted and don't see what's really going on around us anymore!"

Erin rolled her eyes at her brother in mock annoyance. He loved a good conspiracy theory. He would make a great lawyer or a politician when he was older; either that or one of those Buddhist teachers surrounded by monkeys in a temple in the middle of a rainforest. That would work! A perfect balance for Lyndon to connect with nature and animals whilst imparting all that wise knowledge he somehow possessed at such a young age.

Stop thinking about what Lyndon will do when he is older! You're as bad as Mum, torturing yourself about the question mark over his future, she scolded herself.

"It's like you, just now. You went straight for my pawn, Erin, and then left yourself wide open! And it was so obvious. I set you up for it. I just *knew* you would do that."

Lyndon was on a roll...

"And how did I know that? Because you're not in the zone! I can see you checking your phone every few seconds! Totally not on alert, which makes you a super easy target. Remember what Dad always says: 'Life is one big chess game; you've always got be on guard because someone might just switch tactics.' I mean, look at the way those dudes Dad has to hang out with stab each other in the back all the time."

Erin pulled her standard grimace in response. They had both witnessed far too many awkward cocktail party scenes in the last year to take any of their dad's political friends seriously. She yawned again and leaned back on the uncomfortable, hard plastic chair as she let Lyndon continue his rant about life and game players.

There was a time, not so long ago, when she would have launched into a counter-attack, often out of resentment of his wiser-than-his-years insights, but not anymore. Now she just wanted to be with him, in this moment, appreciating all the things that made him her little brother. The boy who, at six years old, knocked his two front teeth out and pushed them back in again without telling anyone. The boy who left notes on their mum's pillow saying she smelt of mummy strawberries. The boy who squared up to the scariest kids in kindergarten when they threatened to squeeze the class hamster until it couldn't breathe. Lyndon was one-of-a-kind.

As much as it pained her—and her ego—to admit it, he really was something special. Mum and Dad must have been in a good mood the day they made him. God knows what they had been drinking when they made her.

Dammit! Erin scolded herself. And damn her stupid reactions too, with all those crazy electrons jumping and falling about! Maybe she had been too reactive last night when she had overheard her parents' kitchen dilemma. *Of course,* her parents would grasp any chance they could to save their genius child, even if it made her sick to contemplate what saving him could entail.

But then, maybe it was *her* overreaction to what she had seen as her father's betrayal of her mother that was the real crime.

Why did she send that photo to Kieran? She had fallen right into his trap and given the master of puppets the ultimate power! He certainly hadn't wasted any time before reacting:

Wow, Erin! What are you trying to do to me?

And then he saved it! The worst kind of betrayal. Erin had typed back straight away.

Hey! Did you just save that? Hope not... Was supposed to be FYEO! Pls delete it! Glad you liked it though. Erin x

But did the M.O.P delete or send her a reassuring message back? Of course not! Where would the fun be in that?

Instead, he left her to squirm in fear and embarrassment, tossing, turning, and basically freaking out all night, driven to near insanity by incessantly checking his social media profiles in case he had posted it anywhere.

"Check mate again!" Lyndon made a sudden squeal of victory as Erin picked up her phone again.

Erin rolled her eyes at him, even though she knew he was making a valid point. Being a slave to her phone—to *him*—did make her a loser. But still, she couldn't resist it anymore. She swiped right to check Kieran's story. He had updated it—a video of one of his skate flips! He must be at the skate park on the South Bank now! It would only take her ten minutes to get there if she walked very fast—or ran!

"Sorry, bro! Gotta run. I'll pop back tomorrow. Same time, I promise!" She squeezed Lyndon's arm and then gathered up her jacket and school books in a haphazard scramble. They only served to slow her down as the books fell back onto the bed again.

"Remember, sis! You gotta think of the game plan. Even Mariola knows that, and she can play chess better than you. She beat me three times yesterday, and she's a more annoying glory hunter than I am. She kept singing that song you like from *Mamma Mia* about a winner taking it all. That's what I got from her *all* afternoon."

Erin shook her head at him. "Oh my God, Lyndon. We need to get you back to school. Singing ABBA with your nurse! You'll be singing to *The Sound of Music* next if we leave you in here any longer. See you later."

Closing the door to her brother's room, she trotted as fast as she dared down the hospital corridor, waiting until she reached the main exit before breaking into a full-speed run.

She needed to get to Kieran. That photo needed deleting. He couldn't win this one. If she let him, he really would be able to take it all.

Trying to run through a swarm of over-heated tourists in the middle of June attracted, rather than deterred attention. She may as well have worn a sign on her head saying, "Stop me and ask me to take your photo."

Normally, Erin would have obliged and done her best to pose a stranger's phone at the ideal angle: the classic Big Ben in the background, captured through the spindles of the London Eye. But not today. Erin shook her head and waved away the out-stretched hand clasping an iPhone in front of her. She couldn't afford to point a random phone in the wrong direction to where she needed to put her own focus.

Two more interruptions slowed her down. First, an excitable Bette Midler look-alike asked her for directions to the Queen's house. Then a bare-chested guy on a unicycle attempted to wow his crowd by circling around Erin whilst singing something in Italian, which sounded deliberately out of tune.

His obstructive wheelie-dance stopped her in her tracks. She took a deep breath, looked around at the beaming faces of holidaying families, and then growled a loud, throttling sound. It was a noise full of deep frustration, one she had no idea she was capable of making. The unicyclist flinched in shock and lost his balance, causing him to fall face-first into a group of colourful lycra-dressed men who had just appeared, giving Erin her chance to escape. It would have been funny if she wasn't so terrified of missing her opportunity to find the man who held the strings to her fate.

The skate park was nearer to the hospital than she remembered. Erin could already see the Royal Festival Hall on her right, with the iconic graffiti-adorned undercroft underneath. The familiar whooshing sound of wheels moving at high speeds up and down concrete ramps was now audible. She stopped, pausing to catch her breath and shake out her t-shirt, which had become stuck to the moist layer of sweat on her back. She momentarily considered walking over to the restaurant opposite, so she could apply some make-up from her bag and spray on some deodorant, but then turned back to the smell of testosterone that she knew needed urgent confronting. It was unlikely she was sweatier than any of the guys in there anyway.

Erin spotted Kieran's helmet immediately. It was a shiny white one, half-covered with his favourite emblem: snakes entwined around two samurai swords and a blue thistle at the top, a nod to his Scottish roots. He had commissioned the logo for himself, to match the tattoo on his back. He called it "Kieran branding" to remind himself that he is a warrior and can never be beaten. It had impressed her when he had told her that at first, even allowing herself to consider the future possibility that she could get a matching one. But that was stupid. Apart from being highly arrogant, she had a pathological fear of snakes!

Kieran must have sensed her presence somehow. He looked over his shoulder at her, a dark expression clouding his face. The look in his eyes told her everything she needed to know. Her heart sank, an embarrassed assault of disappointment rushing through her. She turned to run away, tears already threatening, but then he called her name out.

"Erin! Come over here! Look at what my mate, Ash, found!"

The relief was overwhelming. Erin had to stop herself from running over to where he was standing next to an alarmingly tall, skinny man who was moving his fingers around in a rave-type dance motion in front of his face. She didn't recognise him from any of Kieran's posts.

From a distance, he looked younger than Kieran. He had certainly made efforts to perfect a "look". His bleach-blond hair had been pulled into a high man bun, which fully exposed an extreme, darker-haired under-shave. As she got nearer to him—close enough to see the deep lines on his forehead, grey bags under his eyes, and sunken-in cheeks—she realised he was probably even older than Kieran. He looked in worse health than some of the patients on Lyndon's ward! He also looked ridiculously out-of-place amongst all the much younger, athletic teenage boys skating around him. Although, so did Kieran.

"Ash, meet Erin. Erin, meet Ash," Kieran mumbled, shifting on his feet and avoiding all eye contact with her.

Ash laughed loudly, punching Kieran on the arm hard. "I see what ya mean," Ash sneered.

Kieran backed away from Ash's punch and folded his arms into his chest defensively. Or maybe it was to enhance the swell of his biceps under his tight-fitting t-shirt? Ash didn't seem to notice. He was too busy staring at Erin's body, deliberately moving his leering gaze from her breasts to the bottom of the zip line on her shorts, whilst chewing noisily on what she could only assume was gum. It was a sickening look that made her feel violated. She could easily have believed he had practiced it in front of a mirror, perhaps in an attempt to win the part of a grotesque pervert in a low-budget movie. He could fit the profile easily.

What are you doing hanging out with this guy, Kieran?

Erin shifted her slouch bag from where it hung at her side so that it covered the front part of her body, turning herself away from Ash's intrusive gaze. She could barely contain her anger with Kieran for not helping her out and moving her away from this hideous excuse of a man.

"Look at what some dude wrote on the wall last night!" Kieran suddenly spoke up, breaking the awkward silence between them.

Erin leaned forward to see the part of the curved brick wall that Kieran was pointing at. It was a white stencilled image of a fat-bellied cat next to the red spray-painted words, "I want to lick Mrs. Donovan's pussy."

"You got any fit teachers with that name at your school, Erin?" Kieran laughed.

Erin shook her head, feeling small and completely out of her depth. She hated this kind of banter; she never said the right thing. The really witty comebacks would always pop into her head a few hours later, when the moment had already gone.

"Ugh, why would someone want to lick a cat? Fur ball nightmare, hey?" she blurted out, hoping her attempt at sarcasm would endear her to this mix of testosterone bravado on wheels. She regretted it immediately. As always, what sounded like a clever response in her head had not made its way into the delivery of her speech.

Kieran and Ash's reactions were identical. Both adopted the same bemused expressions, ones that suggested they viewed her as nothing more than a piece of stupidity wearing a bra.

"Erin! You do know it means vagina?" Kieran bristled. He looked mortified now, like she was an embarrassment to him.

Ash laughed and slapped Kieran on his back in a show of vile appreciation. "Yeah! A nicely-shaved one too. Just like a baby's bum. No chance of fur balls for you with this one, Kieran, eh?" Ash challenged, raising his eyebrows at Erin.

Erin felt her head spinning as she registered the real meaning of Ash's words. Kieran must have shown the photo to this monstrous excuse of a human being. The rage of humiliation was sudden and intense, the wound to her pride alerting her body to react. This was a different type of energy, a release of pure fury. The M.O.P had snapped off those strings and freed her from his control. She hated him!

And she was ready to play her winning card. She may be a lot younger than these idiots, but she was a hell of a lot smarter. Forcing herself to laugh—a fake, probably unconvincing one—she prepared herself to attack.

"And I thought the British were supposed to be masters of sarcasm! But then, I guess that doesn't apply to sweaty, sad old blokes who like to pretend they're teenagers rather than get off their butts and do some actual work."

Ash took two steps towards her and licked his lips in a deliberate, slow movement. It was undoubtedly an attempt to frighten her but one that just made him look ridiculous. Saliva dribbled down his chin. He would never get the part of Hannibal Lector—that was for sure.

"Nah, love, the only thing that needs *working* is this love machine here... and it's little teenagers like you that do the best and *tightest* job."

Check mate to Ash! Now she was frightened. Erin stepped back, looking behind her to check she was still visible to the light of the South Bank and the people walking past. His words crawled over her entire body, like hundreds of vicious scarabs, eating away at her skin and her dignity. The "chicken bubbles" she and Lyndon had laughed about only an hour ago were no longer funny; it was more like welts of terror popping up all over her.

Shooting Kieran a desperate look, she pleaded with him through gritted teeth, "Aren't you going to say anything?"

Had she not meant anything to him at all?

But Kieran just shook his head at her in irritated disgust.

"Go home, Erin. Go home to Daddy. You shouldn't have come down here like some desperate stalker. Just because I put a photo on my

Snapchat story... it wasn't an invitation meant for you."

He turned his back to her then, slamming his foot on the edge of the skateboard so that it could flip up to him from the other side. Then he jumped on with both feet, letting himself career down a nearby ramp, away from her and the embarrassment he obviously felt she had caused him.

Erin didn't hesitate. She ran. The tears came so quickly, she could hardly see where she was going as she pushed her way out of the entrance to the skate park and onto the busy riverside walkway. The urgent need to escape from her crippling disappointment in Kieran, the vulgarity of Ash, and all the darkness they had revealed to her quickly transformed her into a human bulldozer. Like a bumper car, she crashed into people, lampposts, pushchairs, and benches— whatever was her in way. She must have looked drunk, and yet, no one stopped her to see if she needed help.

It was only when she reached the corner of the Oxo building that she was finally forced to abandon her blind run of terror. The crowds were too thick for her to break through. It seemed safe to let herself lean on the steel railings that curved in front of the shops and art galleries. She closed her eyes as she caught her breath. Enough distance had been put between her and the monsters by now.

"Erin! You need to stop running now."

The sound of a familiar voice by her side, one that had addressed her by her name, made her flinch. Erin still didn't open her eyes. It wasn't necessary for her to identify who the voice belonged to.

It spoke again. "You have no need to fear me, Erin. I can help you." Erin turned around to face the owner of the voice and almost laughed when she saw the tall girl with the sharply-cut, dark bob and silver-rimmed sunglasses standing next to her. Of course, this girl— or whatever she was—would appear now. Just what she needed: more madness! No doubt someone else who wanted to take something from her and exploit her or her family in some way.

"My name is Parador. Shall we talk, Erin? I know of your family... and I think you are aware of mine."

Erin sighed. She thought about running again, but where would she go? To her house, with all its security cameras and echoes of abandonment? Back to the hospital and the suffocating sound of beeping machines? To her dad's office and absurd politicians shouting at each other about Europe, using the same sound bites back at each other over again?

Perhaps Lyndon was right. It *was* one big game-playing world. And right now, it seemed as though she was just another pawn. Whoever this "girl" in front of her was, she looked like she had more answers than Erin did.

6

DIAMONDS

I t was colder than before. And darker. Erin lifted her right hand in front of her face, wiggling her fingers as though waving back to herself. She couldn't see a thing. And yet, she knew where she was. Just the smell of terror was enough to confirm that she was back on the damn sinking ship again. Another dream message; another warning. Erin shivered, already feeling annoyed that she would have to endure the treacherous weather conditions in this dream scene yet again.

"Parador! Are you here?" she shouted out.

Two brilliant lights flickered in front of her, confirming that Parador was indeed close.

"Can you see it, Erin?" Parador's voice carried across the howling winds.

"I can see your eyes, yes! Well, the flashing light from your pupils.

But that's all! Can you come closer?" Erin trembled.

"You need to find a way out of the darkness," Parador responded.

Erin flinched. So, this dream was a Kieran warning.

"I told you yesterday. I'm not going near him again. You said he had dark energy, and it had to be stopped. So, that's it. I'm not seeing him anymore. I don't understand why you keep coming to me in my dreams like this. If you're a real person, why do we have to do this?" Erin called out, directing her voice towards the lights that flashed in the darkness.

Parador didn't respond. Erin tightened her grip on the wet pole at the side of her and waited.

"I'm tired," Erin managed after too many long seconds had passed. She just wanted to sleep in peace. To wake up fully rested for once!

When at last a gust of wind wafted the scent of chocolate mint in her direction, Erin sighed with relief. Now she could hear the message and get out of this treacherous dream.

"Focus, Erin! Sometimes the only way forward is to reach back." Erin frowned. The voice that now spoke out from the darkness was filled with anguish, almost desperation. She was not sure whether it still belonged to Parador. It sounded gentler, like it belonged to the other version of the girl, the one with the pink, softer colours around her. The one who had warned her that everything was breakable.

"Are you someone else now? You don't sound like the one I met yesterday. The Parador girl who rescued me from my running spree, who calmed me down after Kieran and that man tried to..."

"Careful with distractions, Erin. The obvious dangers are often not the ones you need to fear," the soft voice interrupted.

"What? Sorry, I don't understand..."

But her plea for answers was lost in mid-air as the ship lurched to the side. Erin screamed as her hands slipped from their grip on the pole. Her cries continued as she tumbled over the wet decking, hitting bodies and boxes on the way. The pain felt real, excruciating. It hurt

so much that she called out for her mum to help her, suddenly terrified that this time she could fall and be lost forever. That this dream
really could become a reality.

Erin woke up feeling woozy and disorientated. She stretched her feet
down and her arms up and then pulled her duvet cover over her
head, already desperate to hide from the day ahead. Adjusting to
reality after one of her warning dreams was never an easy task. Particularly when she had been put through a terrifying ordeal like the one
she had just awoken from. Her head pounded in rhythm with her
rapid heartbeat, the hairs on her arms stood on end, and her nose
itched like she had inhaled the dust from an ancient book.

She peeked her head out from under the covers to check the time on
her bedside clock. It was only seven. There was still enough time to
catch up on sleep before school. Relieved, she closed her eyes,
quickly slipping into a heavier morning slumber.

Buzz... buzz... buzz.

The sound of her phone vibrating under the pillow jolted her awake.
She glanced at the clock again. Only seven minutes had passed. Her
head pounded even harder. On automatic pilot, she slipped her hand
under the sheets to pull out the device.

"Ugh!" she groaned when she saw Kieran was calling her. She clicked
the green circle to answer, barely having time to say hello before his
voice boomed through the receiver.

"Hey, Erin! You still cuddling that pink teddy of yours?" Kieran
mocked.

"Erm... I didn't expect you'd call me again. Not after yesterday," she
whispered.

"I'm in bed looking at that delicious photo you sent me! *So* many
hours of entertainment to be had with it too." His voice was a deliberate sneer. It was unrecognizable to her now.

"Kieran, can you delete it, *please?*"

The sound of his malicious laughter made her squirm. She buried herself even further under the duvet.

"Not a chance, Erin! That photo is priceless. I mean, I would've preferred a close-up! *But...* it'll be easier to make some money out of it this way, what with your face showing in the reflection of the mirror. Nice one! Thanks for making it easier for me."

Erin gasped. Her mind raced as she tried to decipher the meaning behind his words. What sounded more like a threat?

"What do you mean, exactly?" she finally dared.

He laughed again. "What I *mean*, little Erin, is that a photo like that could do a lot of damage to a diplomat's reputation. And your daddy is an ambassador, is he not?"

Tears filled her eyes. She shoved her fist into her mouth to disguise her sob.

"What do you want?" she managed to squeak.

"What everyone wants in this world, Erin ... money!"

The sight of the gingerbread man biscuit lying on her bed that made Erin vomit. She managed to get to the toilet in her en-suite just in time. The first retches made her cry and call out for her mum, a habit she hadn't grown out of. But then, as she knelt backwards on the cold black and white tiles, her bottom sinking into her heels, she realised it wasn't enough. She needed to get more out, to free her body of whatever darkness she had absorbed over the last few hours.

Erin stuck her fingers to the back of her throat. Her body reacted immediately. And then she cried again. But she didn't call out for her mum this time, nor her dad. What good could they do to get her out of the mess she— they—were all in? She needed something bigger than parental love to overcome the monsters she was faced with, even if she had to resort to pleading with a concept she wasn't sure she believed in anymore.

"God!" she screamed out loud, shoving her fist into her mouth and curling her knees up to her chin in the protective foetal position. The tiled floor was freezing, making her shiver violently. She didn't care. This self-inflicted discomfort seemed the appropriate punishment she deserved for letting herself get into such a dangerous position.

How could she have fallen for such an evil man? She had heard about things like this happening to people, but she never could have believed that she would fall into such a stupid trap. She'd become a victim to exploitation by someone whom she now realised was a vile monstrosity.

Part of her couldn't quite believe that it was all happening, that Kieran was really threatening to destroy her life... and her family... and for what? So that he could buy more drugs and throw his life away? It had to be drugs. It would explain Ash's jittery body movements and why Kieran was hanging out with such a low-life. Why else would he need that amount of cash? Either drugs or those dodgy clubs he clearly had a penchant for visiting.

God, he really had coloured every ounce of her judgment. The very fact that he had boasted to her about his lad's trip to Singapore, where they had all enjoyed a night at the "Four Floors of Whores" should have set alarm bells ringing and sent her running. But no! She had just blindly laughed along with him as he regaled her with false tales of friendly banter and innocent drinks. He had been so insistent, so convincing.

"Nah, Erin! I'm not into all that buying sex stuff. We just had a few dances and bought the girls a few drinks."

Why wouldn't she have believed him? If anything, it had weirdly made him more attractive to her. It was just the right balance of stirring up jealousy and respect. The idea that he had acted like a gentleman despite being drunk amongst a sea of prostitutes furthered her respect—and desire—for him.

Her phone vibrated in the back pocket of her jeans. She wanted to ignore it in case it was *him* again, placing more terrifying demands on her. But she gave in and reached around to pull it out and check. It could be Parador confirming details of their rescue plan. It was!

The message was to-the-point.

All arrangements have been made. Meet me at 2 pm at Gem Bar in Piccadilly tomorrow. Bring one of your dad's empty briefcases. Message Kieran. Tell him to meet you in there at 3 pm, and you will have his money. Plan will be revealed when we meet before he turns up.

Erin sat bolt-upright. She had no idea what Parador was planning. It was terrifying but kind of exhilarating at the same time. Whatever the strategy was, there was no way Kieran could win this battle. Not against someone like *her*! This girl, woman, mystical alien-dream-lady —whoever she was, she could see everything! Erin hadn't even needed to tell her why she was running the other day. Parador had just looked into her eyes for a few seconds, nodded at her, and said, "You have been treated very badly by this man. He has a dark energy. It needs to be stopped."

And then, even better, she had cupped both her hands under Erin's elbows and zapped her! The only way to describe it was like a surge of pleasurable electrical pulses being shot through her body. And amazingly, it had immediately calmed her down. It was an instant pacemaker effect and all from the magic of Parador's fingertips.

Erin got up from the harsh bathroom tiles, moving to the soft warmth of her freshly made bed. She messaged Parador a reply:

Okay. I will be there. I'll message the dark energy guy now. Thank you. E

Good. Now delete this message thread. P

Erin deleted the messages and quickly sent one to Kieran with Parador's instructions.

Kieran replied straight away.

Good. Glad to know you weren't a waste of my time after all.

The message slapped, punched, kicked, and stripped her all in one blow. She wished his venomous words didn't hurt her so much and that she was made of stronger stuff, a thicker skin. But she wasn't. She was just Erin Barrett, a fifteen-year-old human girl with no power to re-start her own heart and no ability to foresee a dark energy in someone who had made her feel so bright.

She wiped away her tears so that she could see what she was doing and quickly deleted the hurtful message from the screen. As she shifted her body to enable her to lie down and bury herself away, she heard the crinkling sound of a wrapper. It made her cry even more when she realised what it was: the gingerbread man biscuit her mum had left on her bed.

"Oh, Mum, where are you?" she whispered as she picked up the biscuit and shoved it into her mouth. Leaving animal-shaped biscuits for her and Lyndon was one of her mum's *things*. It obviously didn't matter how old they both were either, nor which country they currently resided in. Stefanie had kept up this weekly tradition for as long as Erin could remember.

The ginger flavour was exactly what she needed right now too. How had her mum known she would need an anti-sickness treat? Maybe her mum was already developing powers from these "people" she had started interacting with. Like Parador and her abilities, or this man her mum was meeting tomorrow.

The very thought of her mum being taken away tomorrow brought on a new wave of queasiness. She gobbled up the rest of the gingerbread man as quickly as she could.

"Run, run, run, as fast as you can. You can't catch me! I'm the gingerbread man," she sang out loud with a self-pitying laugh.

Well, you can't make me run for you, Kieran! Not anymore! she thought.

A flash of pink caught her eye. She reached down to the end of her bed to see what it was. A note from her mum! It must have been positioned with the gingerbread man— another *thing* her mum liked to do every now and then. It was usually a poem or some lyrics from a song. It was always a little way for her mum to try and connect with them, particularly when she knew she had been working too much.

Don't let anyone dull
your sparkle.
You are a diamond!
But even stronger.
You can never be broken!
I'm always here, Erin.

Love you. Mum xxx

Wow! Why had her mum chosen to mention diamonds, of all things?

Notebook! she thought instantly. What if her mum had been reading her recent ramblings? If she had, she would have read all the stuff about her dad taking her to the diamond museum and how worried she was that *their* family diamond was going to break!

It also meant her mum must know she was involved with Kieran too! And if this were the case, there had to be a deeper meaning hidden in her mum's message, one that she was assuming Erin would be able to work out. Was this her mum's way of saying it was all going to be okay —both with Kieran and with their mad plan to save Lyndon? Was she offering another means to communicate?

Without hesitating, Erin ran over to the top drawer of her dresser, where she had hidden her notebook under her underwear in a rush the day before. Frantically, she felt about under the material of her tights and panties and quickly started to panic when she realised she could only feel the scratchy, wood-splintered base of the drawer. She quickly opened the drawer underneath and breathed out an audible sigh of relief when she pulled out the purple book from underneath her workout t-shirt and leggings.

"Typical," she muttered to herself. Only *her* mum would go on a snooping spree and completely fail to hide her tracks. Erin pulled her hair into a ponytail and walked over to her desk to find a pen, then flicked the pages of her notebook to the last entry.

JUNE 25, 2018

Dear Stefomum,

I tried to talk to the adult you this morning. I wanted to see if we could book that makeover at Harrods you bought me for my birthday. But then, when I watched you stuffing all those clinical trials about Lyndon's treatment in your bag, I realised how self-absorbed that would sound.

And anyway, you were in your usual roadrunner mode. So busy answering the phone, popping those headache pills you store in your handbag like mints, or scribbling down instructions for me and Dad for the day's usual chaotic schedule! Non-stop!

We are all like passing ships in the night, hey? Well, you and Dad are anyway. I am still stuck here, on the desolate shore that is this house, waiting for our lives to start again!

And that sounds really selfish, doesn't it? Jeez, don't I know it! But y'know, even without Lyndon getting so sick, I do wonder if it would be that different. Are you and Dad that happy? I see it, Stefomum. That girl you were in 1995—the romantic, dreaming one. You were still like that with Dad not so long ago. You were always leaving each other cute notes around the house in random places for each other to find—some of them more embarrassing than others!

I guess you assumed we wouldn't notice, but we did. Lyndon and I used to roll our eyes at each other and say how embarrassing you both were, but we loved it, really. I think it made us feel happy... safe! But the notes have stopped. I haven't seen any since Lyndon became so ill. You don't look at each other in the same way or laugh at each other's jokes the way you used to. It's all so intense and serious now, like a crisis boardroom meeting that never ends!

Dad always said achieving the ambassador post was his dream, but maybe it's a case of "Be careful what you wish for"?

Honestly, it's like living in a series of House of Cards, *the way people come in and out of this house and demand attention from Dad or you.*

I'm not sure you like it either, Stefomum. I can't imagine it's what you thought your life would be. You keep writing in your diary about becoming a human rights lawyer in 1995. But twenty years later, and you are tied to being the wife of a politician with only your camera and charity work for escape! Not that I don't think what you do is amazing. I just know you have to put Dad's work first. Sorry to deliver this bomb to you, btw—I am sure my future dream job won't come true either!

But it was easier when it was just the four of us in not-so-important land. Even if Lyndon is in the hospital, wouldn't it all be much easier to handle it if we were a proper team again?

Do you remember when I came home from school when we lived in

Geneva? And I was SO upset because one of the girls had teased me about how boring our surname is? She was English. She said Barrett was a "bog-standard, middle-of-the-road name for boring people who lived in boring housing estates that all looked the same!"

Isabella Diamond—that was her name. I hated that she had such a pretty, glamorous name. I remember thinking if I were called Erin Sapphire or Erin Ruby, I could have had a shot at giving her some kind of gemstone comeback!

Ugh! She was so full of herself and her position in life that was hers through no merit of her own, just a ridiculously plummy accent. I think that's why I reacted so badly when you guys announced we were moving to England. I thought I was going to be surrounded by a load of prissy Isabella Diamonds.

But Dad was a superstar about my Geneva school meltdown, hey. He took me on a bonding trip to Amsterdam to see the Diamond Museum, so I could have a go at polishing a diamond myself. If I'm honest, I didn't really get it at the time. It just felt really random.

Dad kept pointing out facts about diamonds and how connected we are to these stones that grew millions of years before we came into being. He told stories of all the diamond polishers that were killed during World War II.

I know we told you all about this when we got back, but… the really special part of that trip was right at the end of our tour, when it finally clicked why Dad had brought me there. We had to fill in the guest book and Dad signed, in huge letters:

"Thank you for a great tour. The DIAMOND Family"

When I asked him why he had done that he said the most amazing, schmaltzy thing ever, he explained, "Erin, honey, as you've just heard, the word 'diamond' originates from the Greek word 'Adamas', meaning 'inde-structible'. And that's what we are. We are a diamond family, tightly bonded together like the atoms of carbon inside a diamond. Nothing can break us! Tell that to Isabella Diamond! And what's in a name anyway? Only boring people get bored!"

It was such a corny moment, and I did blush as people looked at us.

But I LOVED it too. And it was at that moment that I totally got why you two got together—you both love saying deep, emotional stuff! And even better, he then told me on the plane home that you were the one to come up with the diamond family idea. You even told him you were more attracted to him because of his name—Adam, like a strong diamond!

But then the moment got stamped on when Dad left me in the gift shop to choose a book, and the tour guide came over and totally ruined it by saying, "You <u>can</u> break a diamond. You just have to find its weak point."

And it's these words that wake me up at night these days, Stefomum. What if we can get broken? So many families around us have broken up. I can't bear the thought of that happening to us!

But the weird thing is that I don't know whether it's my subconscious telling me that I've found my weak point, my Achilles heel, with Kieran or whether it's much worse. What if it's our diamond family that has found its weak point?

We just need Lyndon to get better...

DAMN! Her mum must have read it. Although, she couldn't be too annoyed. She was being highly hypocritical even thinking such thoughts of her mum prying on her. It was, after all, Erin who had started this whole thing by reading her mum's teenage diary!

And it was quite possible that her mum was making a point by not putting the notebook where she had found it. Perhaps her mum *wanted* Erin to know that she had read it? And if this were the case, maybe Erin's idea to find a connection with her mum through the pages of time had not been so crazy? She had been so focused on writing to the teenage version of her mum—one that could never react to her—and yet, the real, grown-up Mum was hearing it after all. And in her own way, she *was* responding, even if it was via sugary treats and words that sounded like one of her favourite country rock songs. It was still a branch, a deeper root reaching out to entwine with hers!

It was a dim light of hope, but it was one that Erin couldn't afford to ignore; there was too much at stake.

She picked up her pen and started to write.

Dear Mum...

But then she quickly changed her mind. She crossed out the word "Mum" several times, so it became indecipherable. She didn't want to embarrass her by making it obvious that her mum's sleuth efforts were an epic fail. The worst thing she could do was to break something that was only just weaving together. It was easier to write to the younger version of her mum, the one Erin could more easily mould into what she wanted her to be.

JUNE 28, 2015

Dear Stefomum,

I'm just going to come out with it... I'm in trouble—and so are you. Let's start with you...Ugh! How do I even write this down to you?

You're so innocent right now... in the nineties! From what you've written in your diary, you don't seem to know any of the full-on stuff yet. You're still kissing boys of your own age and watching your sickly-sweet Doris Day movies. I reckon you're drawn to the older, romantic times, when everything seemed easier and more black and white. Well, I can tell you this: It's not even grey at the moment. It's more like one huge blob of coloured chaos that I can't see through!

It's a shame you are not more interested in the sci-fi stuff like Uncle Johnny was (sorry... I mean your brother, Johnny). It could have been good grounding for you and helped you to get your head around what is happening to us all now! Because Stefomum, your problem really is out-of-this-world—literally!

You and Dad don't even realise that I know about what you have agreed to do tomorrow. I think you must have assumed that I am oblivious to it all, that I'm so wrapped up in my own world, too busy being a typical teenage pleasure seeker! Trust me, I know a lot more than you would like me to!

And believe me, I think about you all the time. I worry about you and Dad and Lyndon every day. I just want to feel safe! You've always been so confident, so full of optimism.

No matter how badly a day has gone, you've always ended it with a shrug and your favourite "Tomorrow is another day" line. Well, Stefomum, it really is.

Because tomorrow, you are going somewhere (I don't know where) to spend the day with a "man" from another world so you can save Lyndon! Because he's sick, Stefomum. Your son, the loveliest boy you could ever imagine being a mum to, he's not well at all.

And all you have to do to get the treatment he needs is agree to take part in an "exchange day" with someone from this other world, called Tandro!

I know! You couldn't make this up even if you wanted to. It's complete madness.

How do I know this? Because I heard you and Dad talking to one of them in our kitchen! It made me feel sick. I wanted to scream at you both, "No! What are you doing? Where will it end? Surely, you must realise it's a trap! If you start giving yourself to someone like that, they will just keep on taking. If you let go of all your power, there's no going back."

I know that sounds dramatic, but have you guys even asked these questions?

Will they really save Lyndon? Will they leave you alone afterwards? Will you come back to us as you were before—unbroken, still connected to Dad, to Lyndon... to me?

It's like there are these two massive forces trying to break us, Stefomum: the one you are going to connect with tomorrow and the one I already have done. And they are <u>both</u> trying to exploit us. They've targeted our weak points.

I don't know if we are all going to be able to survive this after you go away tomorrow. How damaged you will be?

And me? This is just the irony—I need their help too! Because I'm in deep water. I've fallen into the most clichéd trap there is. And it's a very deep hole, one I've no idea how to climb out of!

Okay, I'll just come out with it. I did something really stupid. I sent Kieran a photo. It was of me, a personal body area—enough said!

I regretted it the minute I pressed the send button. And now he is using it against me. Kieran is blackmailing me. He phoned me this morning and almost hissed down the phone:"10K by the end of the weekend or the whole world gets to view Daddy's perfect princess and her cat!"

He is mocking me even more with the cat reference... don't even go there. I realise now he must have targeted me all along because of

Dad's position as an ambassador. I was too honest about what Dad does, who he knows, where we live, etc. And this is the price I—or we —have to pay!

You have always said I'm too honest for my own good.

Can you see the parallels, Stefomum? <u>I'm</u> a victim of sextortion, and <u>you're</u> a victim of Tandrortion. I made that last bit up. It's not clever, I know, but it kind of makes sense to me.

You're probably thinking, "Why would someone send a photo of their private parts on a phone?"

It's stupid, hey! I never thought I would be that dumb. In my defence, I was in shock. I was just so ANGRY with Dad when I overheard him agree to let you be used as an experiment! It was a mad reaction, a reckless one. It's just too easy to send a message. I now realise the hard part is erasing it.

I guess I felt let down, particularly by Dad. I mean, can't he negotiate a better arrangement than this? I thought he had power in his position. I assumed he was a mover-shaker.

But obviously not! Tomorrow, you will be taken away from us. I know all about it. I met with one of them the other day. Her name is Parador. She's actually really nice—very human-like, really, apart from the monosyllabic sentences and the crazy, flickering eyes.

Parador told me I didn't need to worry about what this man was going to do to you. She said it is just an emotional exchange thing. You will not be hurt. All you will need to do is wear this diamond necklace that they will give you, called a Derado, and it will transfer some of your emotional energy to this Tandro guy.

I know I am pushing you here, Stefomum, in 1995. It's a bit like those Back to the Future *films. You are watching films from the past, and I am sending you forward to a future even beyond what the present me could have imagined!*

I did feel better after hearing Parador say your exchange day was just an emotional mind-reading thing. Although now I feel even more stupid for jumping to conclusions. I thought Dad had agreed to give your body away for a day! Such a hideous thought—even if it did mean saving Lyndon! I have to just hope and pray that she was telling me the truth.

I just know how much Dad worships you. I so wanted to scream at him, "You're an ambassador! Do something!"

We have money! There has to be room for some negotiation. Surely, someone else could do the deed for you?

But Parador explained why it has to be you. *Apparently, you are an exceptionally deep-layered emotional human. They haven't been able to find very many people with energy like yours! And guess what, Stefomum? Appar-*

ently, my energy is similar to yours! For once, I actually seem to have inherited something from you.

So, yes, I started by saying we are both in trouble, and we kind of are, but if Parador is right, and you are just going to do a little emotional sharing and then Lyndon will be saved, then... you are in the clear.

And back to me. Well, Parador is hopefully going to be right about getting me out of trouble too. She has a plan, and I've decided to trust her. I don't have any other options. I got myself into this mess, and I need to get myself out of it.

So, whilst you're saving Lyndon on your "day away" tomorrow, I'll be saving myself and our family's reputation with the help of Parador.

Funny, hey! I guess it really is an exchange after all. You are helping the Tandro people with your energy, and they are helping to save both your children.

Love, E x

ERIN READ over what she had written. It was probably too much. Did she really want her mum to read what was going on with Kieran? She was about to tear out the pages but then decided against it. She had no idea what was going to happen tomorrow or if whatever Parador was planning was safe. This notebook could be her lifeline. If, for any reason, her mum got back from her alien day away and Erin wasn't there, at least there was hope she would know to look in this notebook.

She quickly picked up her pen and scribbled down some additional notes at the bottom of the last entry.

Saturday – 2 pm – Piccadilly – Gem Bar – Parador

There it was—evidence of her whereabouts tomorrow, only if she needed it to be found.

All being well, she would get home tomorrow afternoon well before her mum did and could rip out the pages then. Tomorrow night, when their lives could all start again, there would be no more sickness, no more weak points.

"Tomorrow really is another day, Stefomum," Erin said out loud. And then she did what she had not done for a long time. She bunched up her knees to her chin, clasped her fingers together in front of her, closed her eyes, and prayed.

7

MIRRORS

Kieran's red baseball cap was easily identifiable above the crowd of people making their escape from the bustle of Piccadilly Circus. She watched him rudely bumping shoulders with anyone who obstructed him as he strode towards the popular restaurant-lined street in the West End.

Parador had instructed Erin to sit at one of the outside tables of the Gem cocktail bar with her glass of Coke and to look busy, which was why she now pretended to work on her laptop whilst she waited for him to approach. She was wearing one of her mum's plain black trouser suits in an attempt to fit in. Even though people often commented that she looked older than her years, she needed to make sure she didn't look suspicious or stand out—perhaps like a terrified young teenager sitting outside a bar!

She couldn't imagine why Parador had chosen such an inappropriate venue for a fifteen-year-old to wait for someone on her own. None of the girls she had met at her school would come somewhere like this, even if the drinking age was lower here than back home in the States.

But here he was now, standing in front of her, blocking the light from the sun that she had been enjoying warming her face whilst she waited to face him. The man she had adored only a week before, who was now her enemy, her perpetrator. Kieran stared down at her with an exaggerated look of contempt, as though he was desperately trying to play a part he had been instructed to play but had no idea how this "character" was supposed to behave. He seemed agitated, his eyes darting around the courtyard space in front of the bar, no doubt to check if she had brought any back-up.

"Pretty weird place to meet, don't ya think? Even one of Mummy's posh suits ain't gonna make you look eighteen," Kieran mocked.

Erin clenched her fists under the table, her nails digging painfully into her palms. Kieran was even talking differently now. It was as though he had been taken over by a different entity. Where was the charming, intelligent man who had smiled at her with such genuine feeling? The one who had told her he had dreamed about a girl with red hair and an American accent only the day before they had met? Who had sung Beatles songs quietly in her ears as he held her?

This wasn't the same man. It couldn't be. He was more like a mean, chip-on-his-shoulder *boy*, the type of lad the teachers conspired against to get him kicked out of school before he did some real damage. It *had* to be drugs that had made him turn this way. Her first thoughts were usually right about these sorts of things.

"I take it you brought the briefcase?" Kieran asked gruffly.

Erin nodded. "I did, but it's in one of my mum's satchels. I didn't want to look too ridiculous carrying an enormous old man's briefcase. As you say, I don't look that old!" Erin answered slowly, taking care to speak her words as clearly as she could, without revealing the fear that was crippling her.

Her body was stiff. A quick getaway from the rigor mortis position she had adopted in the uncomfortable metal chair was highly unlikely. Erin glanced at her watch. Where was Parador? She needed to stall Kieran a few more minutes before he started demanding to see any money.

"Can you sit down for a minute, please?" she asked him, attempting a shy smile. She hoped it would weaken his resolve, perhaps wean him off this absurd attempt to act like some bad guy.

Kieran hesitated at first but then kicked the chair leg near to him to move it away from the table and sat down. He raised his eyebrows at her, as though waiting for her to speak.

Erin coughed to clear her throat. "Look, Kieran, I know I won't see you again after today, but I wanted to say..." She stopped herself. Could she really bring herself to say this? "I'm sorry..." she continued. Yes, she could. These were desperate times.

Kieran looked surprised. He shifted in his chair and shoved his little finger into the corner of his mouth to nibble the hard skin around his nail. He looked pathetic suddenly, as though a filter had been removed from Erin's eyes that allowed her to finally see his true colours. It helped Erin and gave her that bit of extra strength she needed to play out the game she *had* to win. Lyndon would be proud of her.

"What I mean is... I'm sorry for being so naïve and for leading you on, maybe. I wasn't ready to do the stuff you wanted me to do with you. You're a man! Kissing was never going to be enough. I realise that now. But maybe you thought I *was* ready, and my messages suggested that too. I guess I was a bit of a prick tease. I didn't mean to be, of course."

She looked around her to check if anyone had sat down at one of the nearby tables and could be in earshot. It was clear, but she lowered her voice anyway.

"So, I've got your money for you and something extra too," she whispered.

Kieran leaned towards her, resting his elbows on the table. The action made his biceps swell, causing the short sleeves of his t-shirt to rise upwards. Erin flinched on catching a glimpse of his "warrior" tattoo under the black cotton material. The red-forked tongue of a snake peeking out was a sharp reminder of the terrifying lair of revenge Parador had set up in one of the back rooms of the bar behind them. Kieran had no idea what was coming his way! But it was Parador's plan, and no one else was offering any other solution. Erin had to see it through now.

"How did you get the money, Erin? Without Daddy asking too many questions?" Kieran asked.

Erin had anticipated he would ask her this. She was fully armoured.

"I sold my Rolex. I thought it was the best way to cover my tracks. My parents won't even notice it's gone. They're too wrapped up in looking after my sick brother."

It worked. Kieran's expression oozed a guilty conscience. *Good! You should feel guilty!* she thought.

A sudden shadow appeared over the glass table between them—the silhouette of a girl with a distinct bob.

"Hello. You must be Kieran," Parador purred.

Kieran's face was a picture: eyes wide, nostrils flared, cheeks sucked in. It was a perfect response to the alarming energy surrounding Parador. There was no question that she was a disarming presence, her voice commanding and sultry all at once.

"Erin is true to her word. The money is inside, along with her extra present for you," she stated.

Kieran shook his head, unable to look Parador straight in the face, even though her strange eyes were concealed by her obligatory dark sunglasses. He turned on Erin instead.

"Do you think I'm stupid? You've probably got half the mafia back there, ready to beat me up," he growled at her.

Parador placed her hand on Kieran's shoulder. "Look at me, Kieran," she commanded as she leaned forward, so her face was only a few inches from his. She removed her glasses and stared straight into his eyes.

Erin sucked in her breath as she watched them, a strange sense of jealousy niggling at her. Kieran's reaction to Parador's gaze, her power over him, was instant. He looked as though he was either going to pass out or kiss her. His complexion changed from ill-grey to a blushing pink within seconds. Whatever she was doing to him with those flickering eyes, her plan to take over him was succeeding.

Erin didn't know where to look. Watching them was uncomfortable. She coughed as loudly as she dared and opened her laptop to give herself a purpose, a reason for being in such close proximity to two people who had locked onto each other.

Then, without a word from either of them, not even a nod or a good-bye, Parador and Kieran walked away from the table and into the darkness of the bar. It felt like an insulting anti-climax, as though she had been left outside from a party she didn't want to go to, but the absence of an invitation stung nonetheless.

Erin felt her whole body sink into the chair as she watched them leave her. There was nothing more she could do now. She could only go home and wait for Parador to send her the video, the evidence that Kieran and his dark energy had been well and truly zapped.

The message from Parador flashed up on the screen of Erin's phone at exactly six pm.

Watch this video now. Do NOT attempt to save. It will automatically delete in exactly 15 minutes.

Erin's hands started shaking. The prospect of watching what had happened between Kieran and Parador in the room at the back of the bar was terrifying. She knew only too well after the events of this week that she could never unsee what she has seen. And she really wasn't sure she was ready to see what was on this video.

But time was of essence. She didn't have the luxury of choosing whether or not to expose herself to the nightmares of a horror movie. She was, in her own way, playing one of the main parts.

She plugged her earphones into her phone, so she could contain the sound from the video to her ears only. Her dad had just returned home, and she could hear him running up and down the stairs outside her door, busying himself with chores that he probably didn't need to do. He was clearly trying to distract himself from thinking about what his wife must be doing with her Tandro man at any given moment, on this doomsday in the history of the Barrett family. Erin could only be grateful that he was unaware that his daughter had *also* spent this day engaging with Tandro powers. The threat to his marital bonds was more than enough for him to contend with. He didn't need to hear his teenage daughter had also been led astray.

It was unlikely he would be alerted to anything suspicious. As always, her dad had just accepted her text message to say she was meeting friends in the city for a bit of shopping for the afternoon; no questions asked. Even so, she had locked her bedroom door to be on the safe side.

Erin pressed play.

Within seconds, her hands started to shake as she struggled to absorb the extraordinary images on the screen. At first glance, there appeared to be *five* Paradors standing in front of Kieran, who was slouching rather awkwardly on a silver, throne-style chair in the centre of a dimly-lit room.

"What can you see, Kieran?"

The voice was unmistakably Parador's, but it wasn't clear which of the five versions of her had spoken. Erin could only just make out Kieran's profile. He was rolling his head from side to side as though struggling to keep awake. Erin wondered if Parador had given him something, a drug of some kind to induce him into a hyper-relaxed state. He wore a fixed, horizontal smile as he slowly moved his gaze across each of the curvaceous figures in front of him.

Erin frowned. She knew there was a bigger plan about to play out, but so far, it looked as though Kieran was enjoying himself a little too much. He, no doubt, thought all his birthdays had arrived at once!

The screen temporarily went out of focus. Erin squinted her eyes to adapt to the movement of the camera as it altered to a wider shot of the room. An abundance of questions raced through her mind. She couldn't understand how Parador had multiplied herself unless she was, in fact, one of five quintuplets? Or perhaps the bizarre imagery was just another element to her Tandro trickery.

There was certainly something of an illusion about the room setup. It was small, circular, and sparsely furnished, with only a few candle-lit tables and red velvet stools positioned randomly near where Kieran was sitting. But it was the position of the wall-to-wall mirrors that really drew her attention. All of them curved outwards, like the convex glass effects in a circus's hall of mirrors, the ones designed to confuse people by reflecting distorted, skinnier versions of themselves.

The five Paradors, all statuesque figures, both in their pose and their rigid stillness, suddenly moved. It was only then that Erin realised there was, in fact, only *one* Parador in the room. She was just somehow reflected in all of the five mirrors facing Kieran. At least it seemed that way. It was hard to tell. Erin even pondered the surreal idea that Parador was somehow *inside* the mirrors!

Kieran groaned. He moved his mouth in a manner that suggested he was trying to speak. The mumbling noise that he did eventually make was barely audible. Erin paused the screen and quickly rewound it a few seconds to try and hear what he had said.

"I see you," he seemed to mutter.

Erin felt her heart thumping in her chest. She glanced at the top of her phone to check the time. There were only ten minutes remaining before the video would delete. When was Parador going to get things going?

Kieran's head slumped to the side, suggesting he had fallen asleep. The five Paradors spoke up loudly, a chorus of voices a split-second apart, causing an echo effect to their speech. "Look into the mirrors, Kieran. I have seen enough to know what you really want now, how you like being taken into another world. Let me take you into our world."

And then the beats began. Loud and low, thumping ceremonial bangs on distant drums, reminiscent of a tribal gathering Erin had witnessed in Kenya a few years before. Erin pressed the side button on her phone to turn the volume down. Kieran's head snapped up. Parador—or all five of her—had his attention again.

The Parador in the middle moved forward, twisting her body sideways as her right hand reached out to the glass that separated her from the room. Her fingers, now glowing with the red-orange burn of a hot iron, penetrated the solid barrier, melting through the vertical plane of glass she clearly wanted to get through. She looked like she was drawing back a curtain in front of her.

The mirror lit up in response to her touch, a reaction that revealed an opening or portal of some kind, wide enough to allow her to step out of the mirror and into the room itself. The other four Paradors morphed into hollow apparitions behind her before disappearing completely.

"Jesus!" Kieran cried out. His feet scraped the floor as he arched his back, clearly frightened by the paranormal display in front of him. The chair didn't move despite his efforts to distance himself from the intimidating figure that was now moving towards him.

This solid Parador stopped a few feet in front of Kieran and stared at him. The flicker of her brilliant pupils cast out vibrant light into the darker setting of the room.

"You like pussy, Kieran?" Parador asked him.

Kieran nodded. Erin could only see the back of his head now, but she could tell his physical response to Parador's question was full of enthusiasm. Her obvious sexual reference immediately distracted him from his initial fear.

"Would you like to see what one looks like on an alien girl like me? It is one of your biggest fantasies, is it not?" she asked.

Kieran sat up straighter and leaned his body towards Parador. "Hell yes!" he answered hoarsely.

"*Okay*, you can play, Kieran—if you really desire—but *first*, I need to access something from *you*."

Parador raised both her arms above her head, clenching both her hands into fists as though she were holding tightly to something inside of them. She wriggled both her wrists in the style of a Bollywood dancer and then released her fingers from her grip to reveal two large, clear, crystal stones.

"These are my markers, Kieran. Have you seen diamonds as big as these before?" she asked him, moving them both around to her front to hover them near his face.

Kieran shrugged his shoulders. "Er, no!" he answered. He sounded impatient.

Erin recognised what Parador was holding immediately. They were octahedron rough diamonds—un-cut diamonds that looked like two pyramids back-to-back. Her dad had bought her one in Amsterdam and had it placed on a chain for her. It was her favourite possession.

Adam had been impressed that his young daughter expressed a preference for owning a diamond that had not been cut in any way, exactly as nature had intended it to be found. Erin remembered the moment so well. It was one of those press-the-pause button moments in her life. She had teased him that she was a cheap date and that her mum would have gone for a more expensive, intricately cut diamond. But her dad had just said, "No, Erin, you and your mum are equally special in that way. You can both see much deeper into things. You are able to step outside of what society expects you to want. I love that about both of you."

Erin never wore the rough diamond chain. It was far too precious to her. It reminded her of what her dad had said to her on that trip— that they were a diamond family, and nothing could break them. She kept it safely locked in her jewellery box. It was the one thing she treasured that she *knew* she could keep hold of.

Erin shuddered at the memory now. It triggered a feeling of dread. The penny was starting to drop. Had she been the one to draw these Tandroans to her family? Had her dreams somehow conjured up these diamond people into their lives to test the very thing about her family that she so feared would break? Had she somehow opened a door that would destroy what she valued the most?

Erin quickly re-wound the video a few seconds again. She needed to stay focused. Time was running out. She pressed play again at the part where Parador was pinching the huge rough diamonds in between her thumbs and index fingers and placing them on both sides of Kieran's collarbones.

"Diamonds absorb the energy around them, Kieran—both good and bad. I want to see what you have inside you first before I show you more of me," Parador explained.

The lights in the room transformed suddenly to a blue, ultraviolet light. The change in energy source had an instant effect on the diamonds. They both glowed a deep, burning red.

"Ouch!" Kieran shouted out, wriggling to free himself from the diamonds that Parador still held on his skin. "They're burning me! Take them off!" he pleaded.

Parador made a shushing noise at him. "Just wait a moment longer. It is no worse than the tattoos you have branded yourself with," she said. But then she removed them from his skin and walked around to the back of his chair, leaning into his ear. "Now, if you look in the mirrors, you can see all the alien pussy you want to," she whispered.

The viewing angle on the screen moved position. Kieran's reaction could be seen perfectly as a new image appeared in the central mirror in front of him: a vision of a younger, almost childlike version of Parador. She was wearing a very short, grey-pleated tennis skirt, a white shirt with rolled-up sleeves, and white tennis trainers with lace rimmed ankle socks. Her hair was braided in French plaits on either side, and she rocked her hips from side to side as she sucked a lollipop. It was more like a sexy schoolgirl look than a childlike one, Erin quickly realised—yet another of Kieran's favourite fantasies.

Erin shook her head in disbelief. The other Parador—the main, solid version—was nowhere to be seen now. She had no idea if this Parador had gone back into the mirror, or if this "schoolgirl" version was just another illusion. Neither option fit in the normal realms of possibility.

Kieran's jaw dropped as he watched this new image of Parador with an open-mouthed gawp that made him look desperate. It made Erin feel cold. What could she ever have found attractive about him? He had seemed so full of power before; now he just looked like a sick pervert.

The beats were still pounding somewhere in the room but getting faster now. "Schoolgirl Parador" matched her hip-swaying move-ments in time to the rhythm of the drums, moving her hands up to her skirt so that the material rose up and down intermittently. It was clearly designed as a deliberate tease for Kieran as each time, it revealed a bit of her lacy red thong.

Then, almost as though on cue, the banging of the drums stopped. The vision of Parador froze, smiled at Kieran, and then turned around so that she had her back to him. Slowly and carefully, she then moved her fingers up the sides of her thighs, jutting out her bottom as she did. She slipped her hands underneath her skirt and pulled down the red thong.

Kieran looked as though he was going to explode. His bottom was raised just above the throne chair, as though he were about to catapult himself into the mirror to get to her.

"Meow," Parador purred at him.

The sound was so realistic, yet so absurd in the context of what was being played out in the scene that Erin actually turned her head to her open bedroom window to see if a stray cat had somehow climbed in.

But then, when she looked back at the screen, she remembered Parador's plan. The cat noise made perfect sense. Just at the very moment that Parador's red thong reached her ankle, a huge, furry, black tail flipped out from under her skirt.

Kieran nearly jumped out of his seat. "What the..." he cried out. "That is not sexy at all!"

Parador swung her whole body around and laughed at him, holding on to the bushy black cat tail, which was swinging wildly around her.

"You have a darkness in you, Kieran. My diamond markers showed me. But I already knew that about you. You like teasing pussy out of young girls like Erin, do you? Well, look in the mirror now and see what you are," she challenged, letting go of the tail and folding her arms across her chest.

The screen went dark for five long seconds. The sound of Kieran's frantic, panicked breathing was all that could be heard. Then two red, diamond-shaped glows appeared in the centre of the room.

"Wow," Erin breathed as she realised the red lights were emanating from Kieran's skin, where Parador had re-branded him earlier.

Without warning, the five mirrors all lit up one by one, illuminating Kieran's terrified face. His eyes were wide and wild-looking. His body movements suggested he was desperately trying to free himself from the chair but was being held back by some unknown force.

"Look in the mirror, Kieran," Parador's voice boomed out from somewhere unidentifiable.

Erin gasped as she looked first at Kieran's shocked face and then at the mirrors in front of him. It was Kieran's reflection looking back at him but a much older version, one that showed deep frown lines, sagging cheeks, and heavy eye-bags. He had lost most of his hair, apart from a few grey whisps that sprayed across his scalp. There were dark brown age spots scattered across his forehead and cheeks, and he had a large goiter protruding from his neck. He had to have aged at least fifty years in this reflection.

Parador had read into his weaknesses perfectly. Erin couldn't help herself; she laughed out loud. She knew how much Kieran feared the prospect of getting older. He had once told her he looked so good for his age, it was unnecessary for him to worry about settling down. When she had teased him about it afterwards, his look of outrage had made her flinch in fear that he might actually hit her. It was another warning sign she had foolishly missed.

The old man in the mirror started to cough. It was the signal Erin had been waiting for. The grand finale had finally arrived.

Kieran looked confused, as though waiting to see if he should be literally mirroring the reactions of the older version of himself. It didn't take long. Soon, they were both coughing, deep, raspy, hacking coughs, as though something was stuck at the back of their throats.

It was the young Kieran—the one she knew—who reacted first, sticking his fingers into the back of his throat to pull at something in there. Erin could hardly breathe. She felt as though she was experiencing the lack of oxygen along with him. Kieran's face started to turn blue as he stuck his fingers further into his mouth, standing up now as he writhed around to relieve himself of whatever he needed to get out of his mouth.

"Fur balls are a pain, hey, Kieran?"

It was Parador. She was back in the mirror again, dressed in her signature black playsuit and waterfall coat. The elderly Kieran had gone.

Kieran ran over to the mirror, banging at the glass with one hand, the other still in his mouth. Parador shook her head at him. It was clear the glass barrier between them was not going to break.

"Just give it a pull. These things always have a way of coming out," Parador suggested, her arms folded now as she watched him with a bemused expression.

Kieran gave another cough and finally pulled his hand forward out of his mouth, bringing with him a thick rope of black fur. He slumped onto his knees, both hands pulling at the rope-like fur ball inside his mouth, desperate to get it all out.

Erin looked at the clock on her phone again. Time had nearly run out, yet she didn't know how she wanted it to end anymore. She just needed to know that it was all over, forever.

At last, when Kieran had pulled out at least two metres of black cat fur from his mouth and collapsed onto the floor in a flood of tears, Parador turned her face to the screen, to address Erin.

"This pussy won't be playing silly games anymore, Erin. If he ever tries to reveal his darkness like that again, to you or anyone else, he will find he has to get something much worse out of his throat. Those diamonds I marked him with have absorbed his dark energy. But they *will* come alive again if they need to. They will show him his true reflection. Because that's the magic of diamonds. That's what diamonds do."

The screen went blank.

Erin burst into tears. Her whole body convulsed as she shook off all the osmosis of darkness that being around Kieran had created in her life: terror, heartbreak, and shame.

She let herself release everything that had been eating her up, and she cried out loud, not even caring if her dad could hear her or not. It was over now. Kieran could not hurt her anymore.

A heavy, frantic knocking sounded from the other side of her door, making her jump. It was her dad:

"Erin! Honey, open the door! What's wrong? Please, honey, open the door now!"

She didn't hesitate. She rushed over to her door, unlocked it, and flung her arms around him.

"They're not going to break us, Dad," she cried into his arms.

"What do you mean, honey? Who isn't going to break us?" Adam asked.

Erin buried her head into the concave of his chest and mumbled, "No one, Daddy. Just like you said. No one."

8
POEMS

"Remember to look up at the stars, not down at your feet," Erin recited without needing to glance at the photo card stuck next to the mirror she was standing in front of. She knew every word displayed on this wall. She could recite every motivational quote written on the little cards her mum had stuck onto the walls and door in their downstairs bathroom.

"Thank you, Stephen Hawking!" she muttered to her reflection. That used to be her favourite quote. Now things were different. Now Erin didn't want to think of anything that could remind her of space —*or* things that could exist out of this world.

"They *do* exist though, don't they, Erin!" she mocked her reflection, correcting her own thoughts in her newly adopted monotone voice.

Her shoulders felt weighed down by something she couldn't see. It made her feel tired and encouraged the feeling that she must lie down again or find some other way to release herself from this invisible pressure. It was like an extra gravity force was pulling her down.

"Erin! Are you talking to yourself in there?"

It was Lyndon. She rolled her eyes at the mirror. He had become so protective of her since he had come out of hospital, never wanting to leave her side. How the tables had turned!

"I'll be right out!" she reassured him in a voice loud enough for him to hear but deliberately low in enthusiasm.

As much as she loved spending time with her brother and was grateful that he was alive and had a bright future ahead of him, she couldn't face adopting the happily-ever-after role disposition he seemed to expect from her these days. And why wouldn't he expect that from her—from all his family? Lyndon still had no idea why he was suddenly cured of a strange disease that had left every senior consultant in both London and New York flummoxed. All he knew was that he was one of those anomalies—the rare terminally ill patient whose body just got better all on its own!

In many ways, it did all look like a happily-ever-after. Lyndon had survived. Her parents were still together—only just. And her psychotic ex-boyfriend, who had been trying to bribe and exploit her, had vanished from her life. The future *should* look promising.

And yet, it just didn't. It looked exhausting. Erin wasn't even sure she had the strength to face whatever mountains she still had to climb. She was only fifteen years old, yet she suspected she had experienced more craziness than most fifty-year-olds! It didn't seem possible there could be more challenging obstacles ahead that she hadn't already conquered. And yet, she *knew* that this was only the beginning.

The dreams that still plagued her promised her as much.

"The future belongs to those who believe in the beauty of their dreams," she mocked, quoting words originally spoken by the late First Lady that she knew were stuck on the door behind her. "What do you think, Eleanor Roosevelt? Hmmm... does my future belong in dreams that taunt me with cats crawling over me and choking me?" she spluttered. Even thinking of the new scenes in her nightly journeys made her cough with revulsion.

Still, her outburst shocked her, as though the girl in the mirror was someone else talking back to her. Her words didn't seem to belong to the girl she once knew herself to be. It was as though she had transformed into a different, older girl—woman, even—who talked to her reflection about the philosophy behind the quotes belonging to famous scientists and politicians.

Scowling at her reflection, she growled, "This is ridiculous!" Turning to face the bathroom door, she grabbed the door handle, ready to join Lyndon in the kitchen before he teased her about having a bowel problem. She *had* been in here for nearly an hour!

Just as she was about to yank the door open, a photo of a child holding the hand of an adult caught her eye and stopped her in her tracks. This was the first time she had seen this photo quote card. Leaning forward, she gasped as she read the title of what appeared to be a poem. She could not imagine when her mum had added this one to her collection or whom she had intended it for—Erin, Lyndon, or all of them?

"Children learn what they live!" she croaked as she read out the words. Using her index finger, she traced the words from left to right.

If a child lives with criticism, he learns to condemn.

If a child lives with hostility, he learns to fight.

Erin frowned as she absorbed the meaning of the words, nodding in agreement at the sentiments, particularly the more positive ones at the bottom, which referred to children who live with fairness also learning justice. That one she could attribute to both her parents. But it was the line in the middle that jumped out at her the most.

If a child lives with shame, he learns to feel guilty.

Erin shook her head as she read this out loud. That was something her mum and dad had never made her feel. They had made it their mission to instill confidence in both her and her brother. But she did know someone who *had* been made to feel like that during her younger years: Stefomum!

Grabbing her school bag from where she had flung it on the bathroom floor, she yanked open the door and turned right—the opposite direction to Lyndon and the smell of hot chocolate emanating from the kitchen. Instead, Erin walked towards the den in the basement, her favourite hide-out when she needed to be alone to gather her thoughts.

The poem on the door—a new addition to her mum's normally super positive collection—had reminded her of something she had seen in her mum's diary. She had been meaning to come back to it so that she could study its meaning more carefully. And as it happened, she had shoved that diary in her school bag this morning, hoping to find time during the tube journey to read it when no one else was looking.

Switching on the lamp on the corner table, Erin slumped down into the furthest corner of the sofa and opened up the diary, letting the bookmark fall to the floor.

JUNE 5, 1999

This diary is nearly reaching an end, which is appropriate as I think a new cycle of life should soon begin for me. I know I have to make these new beginnings. There is no use waiting for them to happen.

Almost every pillar in my life has crashed around me. My family is broken. I feel heartbroken, scared, and alone. I don't even know who to blame. Mum says one thing, and Dad says another. I can't be bothered to listen to their reasons anymore. I don't want to know the details. I have heard enough to get the gist of it: an affair!

What a surprise! And they wonder why I want to go away this summer! Why should I let them bounce me between these new houses they have chosen to now live in? It's my life. I want to live it!

I don't feel at home here anymore.

So, I'm going to seek freedom. I got myself a summer visa to work in the States. I'm taking a job as a waitress in America. I'm getting away from here!

Watch this space.

Love, S x

Erin let her tears fall on to the open page of her mum's diary, one by one. How had she never realised just how much pain her mum had been through all those years ago? She checked the date of the diary entry again: 1999. Stefomum would have been eighteen! Not that much older than she was now.

"You must have felt so alone!" Erin hushed in the direction of the words on the page that had been written by the younger version of her mum, whom she so desperately wanted to reach out to—to finally understand.

The coffee table was close enough reach for her to grab a handful of tissues without too much effort. Blowing her nose loudly, Erin curled her feet underneath the blanket and lay down on her back, the diary raised above her head in her outstretched arms.

The date of this entry intrigued her. If Stefomum had gone to America in the summer of '99, then she must have met Adam, her dad, during this time too. Erin turned the pages over quickly, not wanting to give too much thought to the merits of reading any further.

She had promised herself—and her teenage mum—not to delve into this part of her mum's history. But that didn't matter now. A lot of things had happened since she had made that secret pact.

As unbelievable as it was, her family *had* been threatened by an outside force that had nearly torn them all apart—one much more surreal and dangerous than the normal mid-life crisis affair her grandparents inflicted on Stefomum. Erin owed it to both her teenage mum and herself to explore more into the beginning of her parents' relationship. She could always skip over any squeamish parts, which there most probably would be. Her parents can't have wasted much time getting to know each other like that either. Erin had been born only a year after this diary entry!

Her heart pounded in her chest, like drum beats building up the tension in an action movie in anticipation of what the words would reveal.

SEPTEMBER 25, 1999

So, the most embarrassing thing happened last night. I tried to sing! And not just any song either—a Dolly Parton song, "Jolene"! And in one of New York's most crowded karaoke bars too!

Yes, I know I promised never to do that again. I'm blaming the fake ID, which helped me get the vodka tonics. Oh, and I'm blaming Cowboy too, the crazy, scary chef at Johnny Rockets. That's the 1950s-style diner where I have been working all summer, by the way.

Cowboy comes from South Carolina. He is very loud and thinks I am a prudish English girl who is so gullible that it would be a travesty not to tease me at every opportunity!

For the record, he's not a cowboy. I just don't dare call him anything else. It's what he's branded himself as, apparently. Weird!

Well, he was the one who locked me in the freezer cupboard at the restaurant one night for a laugh when I got all scared about the idea of hurricane parties. And he's also the one who told me he heard me singing in the locker rooms and that I was actually quite good!

Well, no, I'm not any good, crazy Cowboy! I'm terrible!

But guess what! It seems no publicity is bad publicity after all! Because... as humiliating as my attempt at karaoke was, I somehow caught the attention of the most unbelievable man!

A drop-dead gorgeous man who didn't even mind that I am a terrible singer. In fact, he seems to like me too—a lot!

His name is Adam Barrett, and he is quite simply beautiful. I clocked him as soon as I stepped off the stage. To say he knocked me off my feet is an understatement because I did actually fall, right in front of him.

Now that wasn't the vodka tonics. It was his voice! I heard him say my name, and it just did something to me.

"Stefanie? Is that your name?"

It was all he said to me! I can't explain why, but it was enough to make me go all funny. It was like he had this magnetic force around him that jolted my body—in a good way! My knees just buckled, gave way, and the next thing I knew, I was sprawled in his arms.

Rachel couldn't stop laughing when she saw it all unfold. She took one look at us together and said, "Well, looks like you guys are in trouble!"

Actually, I'm a bit annoyed with her. She just left me there with him after that, mumbled something about being tired and not wanting to be a gooseberry. But we were in a bar in New York City, and we always swore we wouldn't desert each other!

Anyway, Adam and I spent the rest of the night together, just talking as though we had known each other forever. It was the best night of my life! We walked for hours, eating pizza slices from his favourite late-night café in Little Italy and then ice cream at South Street Seaport. He knows a guy who works at the restaurant who let us sneak in even though it had already closed.

Oh, I should mention that Adam seems to know a lot of people as he's a big shot on Wall Street (yes, I know, I always attract the older guys... but he is different). Adam says he wants to go into politics. That's his dream. He wants to change the world for the better!

He told me then about how he had spent his life fighting to change his trajectory. He never met his parents and was jostled between lots of foster homes. Luckily, he found a mentor in a bank where he worked in Philadelphia who pushed him to get to the Big Apple and realise his dreams! Thank God he did!

I didn't want the night to end. And then, finally, as we walked down to the edge of the water at the side of Brooklyn Bridge, he took me in his arms and said, "Stefanie, I think my life has finally begun!"

I thought I was going to cry! It was exactly the way I was feeling— and still do.

We kissed under the moonlight. I am not exaggerating either.

That's exactly what it was like. Just like the movies.

I think I am actually falling... and it's the best feeling I have ever

had!

Watch this space.

Love, S xx

ERIN SLAMMED the diary together in her hands and let herself cry it all out, everything she had been holding in.

"Thank you, Stefomum," she whispered into the sofa cushion, the diary now clutched to her chest.

This story felt like the greatest gift she had ever received. It warmed her from somewhere deep inside, in a way that no other experience ever had. It was better than the feeling of hot water rushing over her after a freezing cold hockey game. It beat a midnight dip in the jacuzzi their father had installed in these cold English gardens of their residence. It was even more powerful than *that* kiss on the Millennium Bridge with Kieran!

It was enlightening because Erin realized now that she had no choice. She had to embrace what had happened to them all, to see it in all its craziness and let it shape her into something even stronger.

Life couldn't be paused. It moved fast and in unexpected directions. It brought new people into it—even, as unbelievable as it was, new energy sources from other worlds.

Erin couldn't just stay locked in the bubble of a magic moment, like the kiss she shared with Kieran on the Millennium Bridge, or keep wishing he was something he was not. Just as her mum couldn't stay in that kiss by the Brooklyn Bridge in 1999 with her dad either!

They needed to accept the things that had happened to them all and that they had shaped them. They had to move forward.

Erin had changed in these last few months. It was a transformation of a more powerful kind. She could feel it—a burning inside of her, a purpose. Her hands reached to her throat to pull out the diamond necklace her dad had gifted her on that trip to Amsterdam, a memory that now seemed trapped in a life she had once lived and had somehow stepped out from.

Parador had suggested Erin had a superior energy inside her. Well, now she needed to find it —the light that the terrifying but brilliant girl with unbelievable abilities had detected from her. Equally, she needed to make sure that whatever strange energy force these people from this other world had exchanged with her family would not break them. They had to stay the diamond family her dad promised her they were.

To do this, she first had to reach out to one of the people she loved the most: Stefanie Barrett—but of this timeline, in 2015.

Erin reached under her blanket to pull out the schoolbag that was still strapped to her arm. It didn't take her long to locate the notebook; she had made sure to hide it in the secure zipped section at the back.

.   .   .

JULY 5, 2015

Dear Stefomum,

The dreams have always confused me. I have not always understood the messages behind them. But there was one consistent message in them all:

To remember who I am, what I can do, and where I come from.

I didn't understand it at the time. I do now.

I come from two people who were a bit lost but who found each other and then never let each other go. Two people who have been through something no human couple should ever have to face: the threat of losing their child and then being given the impossible choice to save him, via means that they knew could break their relationship apart. It won't though. You are both stronger than that!

Thank you for writing what is happening to you now—sorry, what <u>did</u> happen back in 1999. Thank you for keeping this diary with you all these years. And thank you for leaving it somewhere you knew I could still find it. I know that you know I'm reading it!

I want to tell you three key things I have found within your diary stories, the things that I can use to draw parallels between us, twenty years apart.

1). I feel your pain about the silly boys who hurt you when you were younger, who belittled you and made you feel small.

I have felt this too.

2). I can relate to your decision to not give your body to someone too soon.

I nearly made that mistake. I am so glad I didn't. And even though I have the most wonderful father—and I know you didn't—I feel your pain at how alone you felt when your family broke apart.

Don't worry, we—your family in your future—are not broken. Not completely!

We have received some blows recently. Our human weaknesses have been put to the test. But it is nothing that can't be fixed. And I'll keep doing my best to make sure it is.

So, Stefomum, I think I should close this door to the nineties now and let you continue that part of your journey without me. It's time I reached out to you again in this timeline, the one we exist in together.

I have a feeling the next few pages may be a little too steamy for my reading tastes anyway! Because you have now met the man of

your dreams—Adam Barrett, my father—and this diary timeline points to the fact that you will be making me pretty soon too. Eek!

(I still can't believe you were so young, by the way.)

So, I'll put your diary back where it belongs and leave my notebook somewhere for you to find too. I do WANT you to read this. I wish I could find the words to say them to you in person. And I will one day, I promise.

For now, I want you to know that I love you, Stefomum... ALL the versions of you.

LOVE, *Erin xxx*

9

SHIPS

E rin stared at her brother in disbelief as he shoved a handful of marshmallows into his mouth and then downed a steaming mug of hot chocolate in one go. It was only four months since his "miracle" cure, and he had not only made a full recovery but had clearly been rebooted by some kind of magic charge; one that must have given him a superhuman strength. It was as though he had a permanent imperative energy inside of him that he had to get out.

"How the hell did you drink that, Lyndon?" Erin asked. "I literally just poured boiling hot water on it, and I didn't put any milk in it this time either."

It was the third mug of cocoa she had made for Lyndon that morning, and each time, she had put less milk in to see if he could handle the temperature. Before his sickness and Tandro recovery, Lyndon had been a bit of a wuss in the heated food and drink department, always the last to finish a family meal whilst he waited for it to cool down. It used to drive them all mad! But now Lyndon could finish a bowl of ice cream within seconds without a hint of a brain freeze and consume boiling hot beverages or food without a single complaint.

Much to all their amazement, he even liked the hottest vindaloo curry now!

Lyndon just grinned at her and shrugged. "I dunno, Sis. I just can!"

he answered before reaching across the kitchen table to break off two bananas from a bunch at the top of the fruit bowl.

"And where do you put all that food? I've never seen you eat so much. You're like a new person."

Lyndon just rolled his eyes at her. "Dude, I just spent two hours on the skate ramp. I *need* fuel. I reckon I clocked a few miles up and down that thing."

The mention of the skate ramp made Erin flinch. Their dad had ordered it to be installed in the gardens of their residence as a present to Lyndon, to celebrate his "miraculous" recovery. Much to Lyndon's annoyance, Erin avoided the hideous monstrosity at all costs. The dark connotations with Kieran, Ash, and that cat stencil in the skatepark were never far from her mind. Even now, she dreamed about it almost every night.

There were a few variations of the nightmare. Sometimes she would be standing in a dark corner of the South Bank skate park with a spotlight over her, completely naked and shivering, whilst men of all shapes and sizes would spray her with red paint, laughing and spitting in her face. In other dreams, she would be walking around a hall of mirrors, desperately trying to find a way out, when hundreds of cats would come running towards her from all directions, clawing at her naked skin.

But the worst one was the dream where Kieran kissed her.

It would start off lovely. He would treat her gently and touch her cheeks with sincerity and warmth, looking at her with that passionate hunger that had so attracted her to him originally. But then it would all change. His hands would wrap around her throat, tightening with every thrust of his tongue in her mouth, choking her as she grabbed at

his hair to try and pull him away from her. And just as she thought she could no longer bear it, she would wake up, spluttering for breath, crying out for help.

But no one ever came. As much as Erin willed it to happen, she would never find herself rescued from the tangle of her sweat-ridden sheets. Her mum and dad never appeared at her side, but then, how could they know she needed them? Her cries never released any sound. They were always silent screams. Even the thought of how she must look made her stomach turn. She had turned into a real-life version of Edvard Munch's "The Scream" painting.

"So... Erin, my favourite, loveliest, most generous sister ever..." Lyndon started.

"I'm your *only* sister! Come on, spit it out. What are you after?" Erin interrupted. She folded her arms across her chest as she sat down opposite him, pretending to take a defensive stance. The sound of his pleading tone coupled with the sight of his open laptop on the table suggested that her brother wanted homework advice.

Lyndon put his thumb up to her. "Excellent! Okay, basically, I have to submit a piece about maritime history in the UK, and it can be anything I want it to be. But I have already explained to Mr. Jones that I'm American, which puts me at a disadvantage. So, I suggested a perfect compromise!" Lyndon explained.

"And that is?" Erin asked.

"The Titanic! It sailed from Southampton, here in the UK, and ended up in New York!"

"Er... no... duh! It never made it to New York. That's the whole point. Are you being serious, Lynds? I thought you were the intelligent one too!" Erin mocked him, wondering for a few seconds whether the energy Tandro had given him had messed up his brain cells.

Lyndon clapped his hands together and tapped on his forehead. "Ah... but I am a genius, you see! I am going to write a parallel love story! It'll be a bit like the film in one version. Y'know, posh bird meets third class dude who catches her eye, but then they get separated when the ship sinks... etc. But then, the *other* version shows what happens between these characters in an alternative world, where the ship makes it to New York fully intact! You like it?" Lyndon asked expectantly.

Unbelievable! she thought. *That damn sinking ship!*

Erin couldn't seem to get away from it recently. Only last week, when she had asked her mum to watch the movie with her, Stefanie had burst into tears and mumbled something about the car scene being inappropriate! It made no sense. They had watched that film together a million times before! It was so out of character for her mum too. It was one of her mum's favourite movies.

But then, trying to pinpoint what could trigger her mum into becoming an emotional wreck these days was completely pointless anyway. Stefanie could cry at the slightest provocation. Whatever part of her energy her mum had given to the Tandro people had clearly not had such a positive effect on her as it had on Lyndon. Even Lyndon had suggested they go through their mum's Spotify favourites and change them to some happier songs. Listening to Adele repeatedly was certainly not improving her mum's disposition, and it wasn't exactly helping Erin to recover from Kieran either. Because, if she were being really honest, no matter how badly he had treated her, it still hurt like hell being cut off from him.

Erin had put *Titanic* on in the den anyway, despite her mum's

irrational protests. Then, much to her surprise, her dad had walked in, sat down for a few happy moments with her, enjoying the popcorn and looking like he was ready to relax and chill for once. But it didn't last long.

They got as far as the naked portrait scene—the one where Kate Winslet sprawls on a chaise longue wearing nothing but a blue diamond necklace—and it had all fallen apart. Her dad had looked like *he* was going to burst into tears! She had tried to find out why the scene had bothered her dad so much—he had never been the squeamish type around moderately naked film scenes in front of her before —but he had just muttered something about the dangers of coloured diamonds and how it was good it got thrown back into the ocean at the end of the film! It was the most bizarre behaviour she had ever witnessed in her dad.

And *now* Lyndon had randomly chosen the story as his latest school project. *Is there a sign I'm supposed to be picking up on here?* Erin wondered.

Erin looked at her brother, who was waiting patiently for her to respond to his project idea.

"We are *all* passengers on the Titanic!" Erin suddenly burst out, much to Lyndon's obvious confusion.

"Eh? What are you on about?" Lyndon asked.

"It's something Dad said the other day when were we watching the movie. Apparently, it's from an Irish philosopher. I was just thinking you could use this in your parallel story. Perhaps you could say, 'We all have to navigate icebergs during life. Some of us crash into them and sink, and others manage to anticipate disaster before it happens...'"

"Yes! Yeah, that's brilliant. That would totally work. I could start

with that as an intro and then go on to say something like, 'Here is a parallel tale of forbidden love on a ship. In one story, they sink, and in another, they fly.' Or maybe that's a bit corny? Ah, come on, Erin. You're better at this slushy stuff than me."

Erin snorted a repressed giggle and was about to respond when the intercom burst into life behind them. She looked over her shoulder to see which room had connected with the kitchen and saw that her dad's office light had lit up. Without hesitating, she got up to press the button to see if he wanted anything from the kitchen but stopped when she heard her dad's anxious voice talking to *Parador*!

Lyndon shook his head in the direction of the intercom. "Who's Dad talking to? He's done it again, hasn't he? He's gone and knocked something onto the intercom again. You'd better buzz through and let him know we can hear him, Erin. He'll go mad if we eavesdrop on his phone conversation again."

Erin shook her head. "Shh…I want to hear this. I know that voice," Erin whispered.

Erin was shaking already at the sound of Parador's voice. She hadn't spoken to her since the video recording with Kieran, so she still had no idea what had happened next. It had been driving her crazy.

For some strange reason, the need to check Kieran was okay after the choking attack had been like a compulsion. He had blocked her from all his social media, so she had no way of tracking him down herself, and she had messaged Parador countless times but had not received any response. It was as though Parador had vanished off the face of the Earth.

In fact, that was the conclusion Erin had come to: that Parador must have gone back to Tandro somehow. But clearly not! From the sounds

of the conversation over the intercom, it was evident Parador was still in London since she had just suggested meeting up with her dad at some private member's club in Chelsea.

Erin bit her lip and steadied herself on the side counter. A strange and familiar sense of dread washed through her. Why would Parador want to meet her dad now? She leaned closer to the speaker to hear what they were saying.

"Parador, I have no intention of meeting you or seeing you ever again. We made a deal, and as far as I am concerned, it is all done and over."

"Yes, we did think it was all complete, but I have recently been informed that the combination of your blue diamond energy and my turquoise energy was not entirely adequate to fill our Derados on the day we made our connection. My ruler is displeased by this. This is not a failure of yours but entirely mine, Mr. Barrett. I should have taken more time to understand your unique emotional energy before we consummated our physical connection. I can assure you that with a little more time, you would find an experience with me more fulfilling and enjoyable. We would find a way to compensate you for this extra effort, if you would oblige. Atla has suggested a small blue diamond from our collection as a thank you. It would be worth a considerable amount for you here."

Erin held her breath as she tried to take in what Parador's words meant. She could hear her dad's heavy breathing. He was clearly mulling over how to respond.

"I will *not* do that again, Parador. I don't give a damn how many diamonds you throw at me. You did something to me, to my mind. I know you did. It's the only explanation. There is no way I would have

agreed to do what we did if I was of sound mind. It's bad enough that you used our son's illness to force Stefanie into breaking our wedding vows, but that wasn't enough for you, was it? You had to work your mind games on me too. A double blow to our family.

"And by the way, I didn't enjoy what you made me do. You shouldn't have assumed all men are the same. We don't all just think with our trousers when we are with a woman. There is a lot more to it than that! There is for me anyway. No way! You've already taken enough of me, for God's sake. Stefanie knows about what we did together. One of your stupid fellow agents must have let the cat out of the bag, and now I have no power at all! You've totally disarmed me, and now my wife feels she has every right to run to HIM... because of the excuse you gave her!"

"You didn't enjoy your experience with me at all?"

"No! If I'm honest, I didn't! You were cold. Well, your body was hot — I mean, temperature-wise... but you were cold in your strange way, and that ruins everything. You drained my energy, so screw you if you didn't get enough of it! My colleague, Elaine, told me only yesterday that her son is fighting fit, so there is no longer any bargaining to be done here, Parador. What are you going to do? Make the boy unwell again? Blackmail me into doing it with you again, so you can send my wife even farther into his lair?"

"I see, Mr. Barrett. Very well. You have made your points clear. I will relay this back to my team. You are correct that your own dealings with me should not have been disclosed."

"You're damn right they shouldn't. I only agreed to it on the basis that it would be confidential. I was trying to help save another child, for God's sake! Or at least that's what your mind trickery convinced

me I was justified in doing."

"Yes, but that was only part of your reason, Mr. Barrett. I could see in you that you had a strong desire to experience a Tandro connection as a means of understanding what had happened to your wife on her exchange day. An understandable reasoning, but I should have explained then that this would not be possible."

"What does *that* mean?"

"Mrs. Barrett and her exchange partner share a very intense connection. It is the strongest one we have witnessed for a very long time. It is not something that can be recreated. There was never a chance that I could have shown you that."

"Great! Thanks for telling me that! Just what I wanted to hear. Jeez, you people make me sick. Do you have any idea what you have done? My wife was perfectly happy and connected to her own family before you guys came along. I don't believe for one second that she has some special bond with *any* of you. You just brainwashed her with those diamond eyes of yours. It's evil, manipulative bullshit. I don't want anything to do with any of you. Stay away from me and my family. Go to hell!"

A loud smashing noise could be heard from inside her dad's office. It sounded like one of the glass cabinets had been hit by a flying object, most probably her dad's phone. Erin switched off the intercom button to shut out any more noise from within the room where she strongly suspected her dad would now be in floods of tears. It was not a sound she wanted to hear or let her brother be exposed to either. She turned to look at Lyndon, who was trembling.

"Erin, what the... what's happening? I don't understand? *Who* was Dad talking to?"

Without hesitating, Erin strode over to her brother and threw her arms around him, burying her face into the softness of his hair, which he had chosen to grow longer as a response to being free of chemotherapy. She felt an instinctive need to protect him, to breathe in the aroma of chocolate, banana, and sweat emanating from his skin and breath. What could she say to him? She was only just connecting all the dots together herself, ones that were rapidly turning into a grotesque picture in her mind: a collage of lies, disappointment and heartbreak.

They had all lied to her: her mum, her dad, *and* Parador. It had been about sex all along. Her first instinct, when she had overhead her parents talking to that scary man on the Tandro screen in this kitchen, had been right. They *had* been after her mum's mind *and* her body! Even in another world, this obsession was rife. It ruled everything and ruined everyone. It was almost too much to take in.

Lyndon pulled away from her.

"Erin! Tell me what's going on. I'm not stupid. It sounds like Dad has been having an affair! And Mum too? But I don't get it... what was Dad on about when he said he was trying to save a child? And that thing about Mum having some intense connection with some exchange partner?" Lyndon pleaded. He sounded like he was on the verge of tears.

Erin closed her eyes, not knowing what she should or shouldn't tell Lyndon. How would he feel if she explained that their mum had secured his life-saving treatment by going off with some other man from another world? Or that it now seemed her dad had betrayed them by engaging with Parador too?

Erin took hold of Lyndon's hands in her own and pulled the ugliest,

most distorted face she could think of. It usually made him laugh, particularly when she flared her nostrils in and out repeatedly, but he just pushed her away this time.

"If you don't start giving me some answers, Erin, I'm going to just walk into Dad's office and demand that he tells me. It's up to you!" Lyndon challenged.

That was the last thing Erin wanted. A part of her was raging at her dad. Overhearing evidence of his pathetic male weakness—which it was, however much he had tried to justify his actions as a life-saving mission for another child—was a devastating blow.

She could actually picture him falling off that golden pedestal she had always placed him on. But her dad was probably curled up in a heap on the floor after hearing what that bitch Parador had told him about their mum's connection with her Tandro man. Whatever he had done wrong, he didn't need to face his demons in front of his children right now—and neither did they.

"Then again, to be fair to Dad, I bet Parador used her crazy mind tricks on him like she did with Kieran!" Erin mumbled to herself.

Lyndon frowned at her and banged his fists down on the table in frustration.

"Okay, okay. Calm down, Lyndon. I know it's a shock. I don't know everything, okay? And Mum and Dad aren't even aware that I know *anything.* But listen, even you must have noticed that Mum has been an emotional wreck recently, and Dad has been acting like a wounded animal for weeks on end. I didn't get it either. Like, why they have both being acting so strange, even knowing the bits that I thought I knew. But... after hearing all that stuff from Dad's office, it *is* now all starting to make more sense..."

"To you, maybe, but you still haven't told me anything," Lyndon interrupted.

Erin put her finger to her lips to silence him, desperately trying to clear her mind, so she could find a way to settle her brother. She looked over to the open laptop screen, where Lyndon had written the title to his project:

The Titanic: A Parallel, Alternative Story

"Of course! The Titanic dream! I'm so stupid! How could I have missed this connection?" she cried out.

Lyndon just stared at her, waiting for her to explain. His bottom lip trembled.

Writing! She could write it down. That was the answer. Just like her notebook, her fingers could spell out the painful words when her tongue failed her. Erin budged Lyndon to move across the wooden bench with her hip, so she could position herself directly in front of the keyboard. She started to type.

Version One:

They thought she was unsinkable. Nothing could take her down. She was the Titanic—invincible, just like the gods she was named after.

But she did sink. She saw the warning signs, yet she didn't listen until it was too late.

Stefanie and Adam thought they were indestructible. Like the composition of a diamond, they were tightly-bonded atoms that could not be broken apart, a rugby scrum that could never collapse.

They didn't think anything could break them.

Yet, they did break. They saw the warning signs, but they didn't listen until it was too late.

Erin paused, wondering how she could get to the point Lyndon was waiting for her to reach.

"Erm... *what* were the warning signs, Erin? Come on... tell me why you are comparing Mum and Dad to sinking ships and breaking diamonds," Lyndon pleaded, bouncing his bottom up and down on the bench in frustration.

Erin looked at her brother and sighed. "The warning signs were *you*, Lyndon. You can always break something, no matter how unbreakable you think it is. That's why I'm talking about a diamond. You *can* break it. You just need to find its weak point."

Before she could continue explaining how scared they had all been of losing him, so frightened that it had made their parents make dangerous decisions, Lyndon smacked his finger on the delete button and erased Erin's words.

"I'm not a weak point, Erin. You're not making any sense," Lyndon responded in a strangled voice. He pressed the keyboard with his index finger several times and then got up from the bench, picked up his skateboard from where it had been resting against the dishwasher, and turned towards the glass door that led to the gardens.

"I need to skate this madness out!" he called out to her as he shut the door behind him.

Erin looked at the screen to see what her brother had typed. Her eyes filled with tears when she realised what he was asking her to do. Two simple words:

Version Two

It was classic Lyndon. In a disaster, he was the type of person who would avoid looking at the rubble, always searching for the helpers, the people clearing the way to enable them to go forward. And now he was looking to her, his older sister, to be the one to find them an alternative route.

Erin wiped her eyes and tapped away.

They said of the Titanic, "Even God Himself couldn't sink this ship." He may have tried, but come hell or high water, this ship would not go down.

They said of The Barrett Family, "Even a diamond can be broken." They may have tried to break them, but even an out-of-this-world energy force cannot tear them apart.

Even as she pressed the full-stop on the laptop keyboard, she shook her head at her reflection in the screen. Lately, she had started to wonder if her body had been taken over by someone else—an older person, one who thought weird, deep thoughts and tied together connections from dreams, diaries and real-life demons.

The sound of the front door slamming made her jump. Her dad was on the move again, hopefully on his way to find her mum and sort out this mess their family was in. The radio hummed behind her, the volume just loud enough for her to detect the opening beats to Adele's "Rolling in the Deep".

"How appropriate!" Erin announced to the empty kitchen. "And I thought you had my back, Parador. Y'know, the whole roll in the deep! But it was all just a means to an end. I bet you just wanted to keep me away from what was really going on. You weren't interested in helping

me at all!"

The distinctive drum beat in the opening of the song playing on the radio made her shudder. It immediately conjured up an image of the video Parador had sent of Kieran in *that* room, of the choking and the cats and those consistent drum beats in the background.

Erin froze then as another thought popped into her head, another connection that she had not yet linked together, even as obvious as this now was. Her new dreams! The recent ones. They were not just haunting memories of the revenge video she had seen. They were a new warning, a message, as her dreams always were! How had it taken her this long to piece this crucial part of the jigsaw together?

Pinching the bridge of her nose, she willed her brain to re-play to her the details of what she saw in her recent dreams. Not the Kieran or the skate park dreams—they were always consistent, and no one ever spoke in them. It was the cats in the hall of mirrors dreams that she needed to focus on. The ones that suggested a message was hidden in there. In this dream scenario, she usually screamed when she saw the cats in the mirror.

But in last night's version of this dream, she hadn't felt the same fear. Instead, she had looked at herself in the mirror, folded her arms across her chest in deliberate defiance, and said, "I am a daughter of diamonds."

And that's all it had taken. The cats had just disappeared! And even better, when she had woken up, her face was smooth, not stuck to the pillow case from sweat and tears.

Erin breathed a sigh of relief as it all suddenly became so clear, as unbelievable as it was. The signs had been there all along. She, Erin Barrett, was somehow connected to *them*—and... so was her mum.

Hadn't Parador said they—whoever *they* were—had not seen someone with such an intense emotional energy as Stefanie for a long time and that Erin also possessed this too?

"Jeez! How could I have missed this?" Erin growled out loud.

The whole thing had been planned. Her mum had been *targeted* by these Tandro people. It was all so obvious now. The evidence had been right in front of her. Erin had just not wanted to see it!

Even Stefomum had hinted at a possible connection with another world in her diary. And yet, Erin had just skipped over that entry—

the one where the seventeen-year-old version of her mum had written about the vivid dreams that haunted her, where strange, bright-eyed people kept calling her the daughter of diamonds.

"I'm such an idiot! You even wrote how stupid you felt when your dad called you ridiculous for listening to dreams and fairy tales made by your mad grandma!" Erin shook her head as she considered this. What she couldn't help feeling was her *own* stupidity—or blindness!

"Remember who you are, what you can do, and where you come from!" Erin groaned the words she remembered now from the dreams —the biggest warning of them all! How could she have missed this glaringly obvious sign?

Erin picked up her phone and typed out three messages in quick succession.

Kieran. I hope you always wear the markers of humiliation. Don't ever put anyone through such exploitation again. Remember, if you even try... you will feel the burn and shame. Mirrors never lie.

She sent it, despite knowing it wouldn't reach him. He had clearly blocked her. It was still cathartic—true freedom from the puppet

master at last!

Then the second message.

Parador, I know everything. You must think I am so young and naïve to believe you really wanted to help me. You just wanted me out of the way whilst you and your "friends" played games with my parents' marriage. I don't know why you want to do this to us, or why I see you, or some version of you, in my dreams, but I will find out, and you won't win. We are stronger than you think. I know who I am now.

She pressed send.

And finally, the third message.

Mum, we need to talk. No more diaries or notebooks. Really talk! Love, E x

As soon as she sent this last message, Erin stood up and made her way out to the hallway in search of comfort. She heard Dobby before she saw him, snoring loudly by the fireplace. Leaning into his soft tummy skin, she breathed in his comforting smell. The dog didn't stir.

"What are you dreaming about, then, boy? Hmmm... I hope it's not cats?" Erin mumbled into the rolled-up layers of Dobby's skin. "But you know what, if you do see any, they may just have a message for you! Like, *open* your eyes, goddammit!"

Dobby breathed in deeply and then let out a loud snort.

Erin smiled. As awful as everything was, she felt a new source of energy bubbling inside her now. A plan was already forming inside her mind. In her last notebook to her mum, she had written about closing

the door to her younger mum's experiences, thinking they all needed to burst out of their magic bubbles in order to move forward.

Well, she had done that with her Kieran bubble. That was *the* only way forward in that story. But for her mum, for Stefanie... it was different. Erin had a strong feeling that in order for their family story to move forward—in the best possible way—she had to help her mum reach back through time. Just as the voice in her dream had said.

"What do you think, Dobby? D'ya reckon I can put Mum back into that bubble she was in with Dad in 1999, under the moonlit sky over Brooklyn Bridge?" Erin pondered into Dobby's velvet-grey fur ears.

The dog responded with another snort.

"I don't mean *literally,* Dobby! I just think I need to find a way to remind her again."

With her words echoing in the vast hallway, Erin gave her dog a kiss and then reached out to the staircase banister.

10

POSTCARDS

Where *was* the diary? Erin was sure she had replaced it in her mum's camera case. Careful not to disturb the ordered array of lenses and batteries, she placed the heavy camera back into the box.

"Damn!" she cried, slumping to the floor.

Lyndon was still swooshing up and down the skate ramp outside at hair-bending speeds, and Dobby had not bothered to join her in the mission to retrieve her mum's teenage diary. As usual, she was on her own with too much space and time to think.

"Why can't I just leave it be?" Erin whispered, letting out an audible sigh. The misty appearance of her breath in front of her face was a grim reminder of just how cold this house had become in these autumn months.

Yawning and shivering in the draughty, cold room, she let herself fall down gently onto the dusty rug in her parent's bedroom. Curling up into a tight foetal position, she racked her brain to think where else she could have put the diary.

Just as her eyelids started to drop, the sudden sound of approaching footsteps on the landing outside made her freeze.

"Hey, monkey, I got your message!"

Erin startled at the sound of her mum's voice from the doorway. Her hands and legs sprung open into a star-shape. And for some reason,

this made her mum chuckle.

"You used to do that as a baby. The slightest noise would make you react just like that," Stefanie mused.

Erin frowned, confused and unsure by her mum's behavior. This was the first time in months that her mum had released a sound even close to laughter. Slowly, Erin swiveled herself into a seated, cross-legged position and beckoned for her mum to join her.

"*Mum!* I have something to tell you. Well, a few things actually," Erin dared.

Stefanie nodded at her, kicked off her cream-coloured snug boots, threw them to the side of the room, and then crawled over to sit down beside her.

"Let me guess... you've worked it out?" Stefanie tried, her eyebrows raised expectantly at her.

Erin exhaled loudly. Now she was in a tricky spot. What did her mum think she had worked out? That both her parents had been tricked into engaging in some kind of illicit exchange with *people* from another world? Or... that she and her mum were both somehow related to them?

"Erin? Are you okay? You look like you've seen a ghost!" Stefanie asked her.

Erin rolled her eyes in a deliberately over-the-top manner, hoping to divert her mum's attention away from the question still hanging in the air between them.

"You look tired!" Erin fired back, regretting it as soon as she said it. She quickly followed up by saying, "Sorry! I didn't mean to sound off. But you do look a bit... what's that word you English guys say? Pesky?" Stefanie shrugged. "Well, no, it's not pesky. I think you mean

'*peaky*'. But remember, monkey, I am the worst person in the world for getting expressions right."

The sound of fake laughter erupted from Erin's mouth before she could stop it. "Yeah, that's right. You don't *do* expressions, do you? Remember that holiday in Martha's Vineyard, when you made so many expression mix-ups that Dad said you should write an ironic joke book? What did he say you should call it again?" Erin questioned, desperate to keep the conversation channelled in this safer direction.

"*Pigs Might Lie*," Stefanie replied. Her voice sounded heavy and sad. "Yeah, maybe that title needs some working on!"
Erin mused. "My favourite one was when you tried to describe one of your scary school teachers and you said she was built like a shit brick house!" Erin laughed.

At least this time, her laughter was genuine. She had forgotten this until just now, and yet, this quirk of her mum's was one of Erin's favourite things about her. It was always made funnier by how long it would take them all to convince Stefanie that her version of an expression was just *wrong*!

"I'll ignore that swear!" Stefanie eventually chuckled in response. Erin watched her mum carefully. It felt excruciating to see how much Stefanie was struggling to find her words. Expressions aside, her mum had always been a jovial chatterbox until recently, when Tandro and all its out-of-this-world energy had come into their lives.

"Sorry, Mum. You okay?" Erin whispered, leaning into her mum for a cuddle. The room was still too cold for comfort. Without hesitation—almost *too* enthusiastically—her mum wrapped her arm around her and pulled her close into her chest. Erin sighed with relief at the warmth and familiar feeling of motherly protection she had missed all

these past months.

"I am now that I'm here with you, Erin. It's been too long since we've done this. Cuddled, chatted and... skirted around that elephant in the room!" Stefanie dared, giving Erin a reassuring squeeze.

Erin nodded into her mum's chest, for once not concerned at being too close to the softness of her breasts. Right now, she would gladly regress back into her younger years and climb onto her lap, rather than face the very adult conversation she knew they were about to have.

"Hmm... I guess the elephant is waiting for attention?" Erin teased, her voice barely an audible whisper.

Stefanie squeezed her even harder. "Yeah, I think it's safe to play about with the elephant expression and not mess it up too much. That's one I *should* remember correctly. It was one of your great-grandma's favourites."

Erin frowned at the mention of her late great-grandma. She leaned forward and twisted herself around, so she could face her mum:

"Great Grandma! She must have known about this too. About..." Erin paused, not sure how much to reveal. Then she took a deep breath and let it all out: "The energy exchange people that you and erm... Dad have become involved with. I mean, she *must* have because why else would she have gone on about diamonds and dreams so much just before she died? And the postcards she left for you, from South Africa. Are you still getting them, even now?" Erin rushed out her words as her brain scrambled all these connections together.

Stefanie nodded.

"I got one just this morning. I don't know how she arranged it all before she left this world, but one thing is for sure, Erin… she *did*

know a lot more than she ever let on. And from the sounds of things, you know more than I hoped you did too."

"Can we not talk about that stuff right now? I'm not ready to go there," Erin pleaded quietly.

She averted her eyes from her mum's troubled gaze. It was too painful to face the guilt and shame she already knew would be written all over her face. Now she had opened the door to her mum's teenage diary, she knew how easy it was for someone—or *something*—to make Stefanie feel this way about herself. And even though she now knew her mum was still involved with her Tandro "man" in some way, she still couldn't find it in herself to subject her mum to more shaming.

Erin knew there was a force more powerful than simple desire at play here. She had seen first-hand what Parador was capable of making people see or feel. In fact, the more she thought about what she had overheard on the kitchen intercom earlier, the more convinced she now was that there was a much more dangerous Master of Puppets at large. Her ex-boyfriend was a mouse compared to Parador!

They sat in silence together, holding hands and breathing in a steady, harmonious rhythm before Stefanie finally spoke.

"Do you want to know what the postcard from your great-grandma said this time?" Stefanie asked.

Erin nodded. "Yes! I *do*! Do you have it?"

Stefanie reached behind her to grab hold of the brown leather straps to her favourite slouch bag. It didn't take her long to find what she was looking for: an old-looking, dark brown leather book.

"The postcard came along with this diary of hers!" Stefanie marvelled. "I know! We girls must have a penchant for writing our thoughts and dreams down in books, no matter what era we're born into!"

Erin smiled shyly. There was no need for either of them to mention their unusual time warp diary conversations.

"What does it say? Anything about dreams or how we are connected to them?" Erin attempted, not sure how far to test her loose theory.

Without answering, Stefanie opened the diary and turned to a page where a red ribbon had marked the last reader's page position.

"Read this and see what you think," Stefanie urged.

Erin could hardly breathe as she took the diary from her mum's shaking hands. The pages were yellow-stained and thin, but the writing was beautifully presented. She read out loud.

December 12, 1980,

Stefanie Rose was born this morning. My beautiful little granddaughter has arrived at last! She really is a beauty. Even more sparkling than my dreams had promised too. There is a magic about her. She has an energy inside her that is more powerful than mine— certainly more than her mother's.

I wasn't sure if Richard would let me see her. I know Esther had to beg for him to let me visit. Luckily, for once, my daughter got her way around that dreadful, controlling husband of hers, and I was allowed a good ten minutes to hold her, to breathe in her skin. Oh, her smell! All babies smell amazing, but Stefanie Rose is something else. Her scent is cinnamon and lemon and somehow conjures the taste of a warm hot cross bun first thing on a cold morning. It's sublime!

I stupidly said this out loud, which, of course, lost me a few minutes of time with the baby. Richard told me to stop talking crazy at his new daughter, but I sensed Esther agreed with me. Bless that lovely

daughter of mine. She has never embraced what is inside her, what is inside of all of the females in our ancestral line... that we are daughters of diamonds!

Something tells me—well, more than that, my dreams have warned me— that Stefanie will be different. Her energy is even more emotionally powerful than her mother's or mine or even my mum's or grandma's. As strange as this seems, since I assumed the link to Tandro would be diluted the further down the line...

Erin broke off, nearly dropping the diary out of her trembling hands.

"Mum! She mentioned Tandro!" Erin exclaimed.

Stefanie nodded, her lips tight as she sat upright and stiff in front of Erin. "I know. Read on though. There's more!"

Erin didn't hesitate. Using her index finger, she quickly found her place and continued from where she left.

As strange as this seems, since I assumed the link to Tandro would be diluted the further down the line, Stefanie Rose is the most powerful one of us all so far. Well, since it all began. Since Tiegal Eureka arrived on this Earth. When she met Johannes Smit, my great, great-grandad and made that one connection that transformed everything!

Erin gasped, her tears blinding her from a clear view of her mum, making it difficult to gauge her expression.

"Tiegal?" Erin asked, barely able to speak. She was vaguely aware of her mum's warm, soft hands reaching around hers, gently pulling the diary from her grasp.

"Tiegal and Johannes were your fifth great grandparents. They lived near the Orange River in South Africa in the late 1800s. Maybe I can

draw you a family tree sometime?" Stefanie suggested.

Erin wiped her eyes to clear her focus.

"Okay, but what is this big connection Great Grandma is referring to?" Erin demanded as she stood up to shake her legs out. Sitting on the floor for so long in the same position had brought about pins and needles in her legs.

"Well, she used to talk about Tiegal to me when I was younger. Back when I was still allowed to see her more often, before my silly dad banned her from the house." Stefanie grumbled at the mention of her father. "Anyway, I had forgotten about this until I read her name again in this diary. You see, I remember thinking it was just another fairy story my grandma was feeding me to keep me in the magic

bubble of childhood. But now... I realise it was a *real* bubble. An energy bubble that started all of this madness all those years ago!"

Erin shook her head as she steadied herself on one of the wooden posts of her parents' bedframe. All of these revelations were coming too fast—first, her dad's connection with Parador, and now her mum, grandma, and even herself being connected with this other world too!

"I can't believe you just used the word 'bubble'," Erin managed as she looked at her mum for feedback, hoping she would understand.

Stefanie nodded enthusiastically. "Yes, I read your last notebook entry. It was lovely, by the way. And *I* always think about magic experiences as being in a bubble too. Like when I first met your dad." She smiled at Erin. The sadness in her eyes still lingered. "*But...* the story in this diary refers to the moment when a girl from another world connected to a boy she kept seeing in her dreams, by a river."

"Tiegal? Was she from Tandro?" Erin exclaimed. She felt a sudden rush of excitement now, of power.

Stefanie stood up slowly and raised her arms into the air as though to offer a pretend surrender.

"I believe she was. Apparently, she appeared in front of the boy from her dreams here on Earth—well, South Africa in 1865, to be specific — in a pink *bubble!*"

Erin tapped her feet in a bid to quieten the loud beating of her heart.

"And the boy was... Johannes, yes?" Erin checked.

"That's right, Erin. And that is why your great-gran always told us to remember who we are, what we can do, and where we come from."

And with those words, Erin and Stefanie Barrett walked towards each other, their arms outstretched towards a long-awaited embrace. They held onto each other tight, bonded and strong, now aware of the weak points that threatened to break them but also now armed with the knowledge that is power.

They were *both* daughters of diamonds.

Want to know more about this world and what happens next?

Sign up to my reader community and become a Tandro Team member at: https://www.tandro.co.uk/jointeamtandro. As a member you will automatically be granted access to the Tandro Treasure Cave - an exclusive virtual treasure cave where you can find diamond energy quizzes, character profiles, as well as book and diamond treasure hunt competitions.

Also by Naomi E Lloyd

Intrigued by how the Earth connection with Tandro first came about and how Erin and Stefanie are historically linked with this other world?

RELEASE, Book One in the TANDRO series, is available to buy now on Amazon. See overleaf for more details.

RELEASE

One connection can transform everything.

In the new world of Tandro, in the year 2065, sexual energy is currency and love connections are forbidden.

Advanced psychic abilities that drive her emotional energies to the limit make Tiegal more valuable than diamonds. If her ruler finds out, he will hunt her down. She must keep her passion hidden. Yet she yearns to unleash her powerful desires, explore the intimacy she craves, and find love.

And then she finds it. When an incredible release of energy transports her into the arms of Johannes, the passionate and romantic man she has been dreaming of.

The only problem is, he exists on Earth in the year 1865. And, she has no idea how long she can stay.

As they set about building a secret life together, amongst the excitement of the diamond rush, Tiegal soon learns that experiencing love, when you are from two different worlds means making painful choices.

How can she keep herself on Earth, and protect the ones she loves, when her enemies on Tandro will do anything to get her back?

RELEASE, Book One in the Tandro Series -
A remarkable love story that transcends the boundaries of both time and space.

Info on all my books

www.naomielloyd.com

Facebook: www.facebook.com/naomielloydauthor

Twitter: www.twitter.com/tandro_trilogy

Instagram: www.instagram.com/naomielloyd/

PLEASE LEAVE A REVIEW

If you've enjoyed this book, it would be tremendous if you could leave a review (it can be as short as you like) on the book's Amazon page. I am reaching out to my readers to ask this favour as reviews help me gain visibility and they can bring my books to the attention of other readers who may enjoy them.

To leave a review, here is the link:
books2read.com/u/mYrpod
Thank you!

Naomi E Lloyd is the author of the Tandro series, a fantasy time travel romance series that transports readers to another time and place.

Naomi is a passionate reader and has an avid interest in sci-fi/fantasy stories, love journeys, and diamonds!

Her diamond world is an internationally connected one. She works as a photographer, a diamond philosopher, and a charitable ambassador for YouCanFree.Us, which focuses on rescuing trafficked women.

As part of her charity, photography, and research work, Naomi has been lucky enough to travel around the world, meeting and interviewing fellow like-minded science romantics of the world.

Naomi's diamond passion is about connection—the journeys that shape rather than break us— although her characters do face extremely tumultuous experiences along the way! It is their resilience and determination that makes their journeys so transformative.

Naomi has woven in her diamond philosophy—along with her romantic imagination—to combine her passion for time travel, parallel worlds, and love stories into an unforgettable journey across time and space.

Although born in Yorkshire and a northern girl at heart, Naomi now lives by the historical beaches of Portsmouth, where she can often be found in a café, tapping away on her laptop, or walking along the sunny promenade with her camera in hand.

Find out more about Naomi E Lloyd at www.naomielloyd.com, where you can sign up to join her reader community and gain access to her exclusive Diamond Energy Cave on her website, where fun quizzes, character profiles, and treasure hunts are waiting to be explored.

ACKNOWLEDGMENTS

I have been talking about writing books for a very long time. There are notebooks in my office filled with ideas that date back to the nineties, all through the noughties and now the... what are we calling this decade? You get the idea.

Safe to say, it has been a long-held dream that I often felt was impossible to reach. It is for this reason I feel so incredibly grateful for the support, patience, and unconditional love from my family and friends.

I could not have started or continued this journey without your support and encouragement.

Thank you! *Naomi*

Printed in Poland
by Amazon Fulfillment
Poland Sp. z o.o., Wrocław

50152691R00089